She Became Aware of A Piano Playing A Familiar Melody.

Intrigued, she followed the sound to one of the spacious old rooms on the other side of the hall. She stood in the doorway, surprised to find Kirk at the keyboard of a battered upright. He was playing the old standard, "As Time Goes By."

Natalie leaned against the piano, watching his fingers move skillfully over the keyboard, impressed at how good he was. When he finished the romantic melody with a flourish, he looked up. Their eyes met. Natalie smiled and said softly, "Play it again, Sam."

PATTI BECKMAN

is one of Silhouette's most prolific authors, and has won much acclaim for her interesting backgrounds. Patti was inspired to write The Movie after working on her Special Edition, Thunder at Dawn, which also accurately depicted the movie industry and the Hollywood scene.

Dear Reader:

Romance readers have been enthusiastic about Silhouette Special Editions for years. And that's not by accident: Special Editions were the first of their kind and continue to feature realistic stories with heightened romantic tension.

The longer stories, sophisticated style, greater sensual detail and variety that made Special Editions popular are the same elements that will make you want to read book after book.

We hope that you enjoy this Special Edition today, and will enjoy many more.

The Editors at Silhouette Books

PATTI BECKMAN
The Movie

Silhouette Special Edition

Published by Silhouette Books New York

America's Publisher of Contemporary Romance

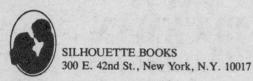

SILHOUETTE BOOKS
300 E. 42nd St., New York, N.Y. 10017

Copyright © 1985 by Patti Beckman

Distributed by Pocket Books

ISBN: 0-373-09226-1

First Silhouette Books printing March, 1985

10 9 8 7 6 5 4 3 2 1

Map by Ray Lundgren

Silhouette, Silhouette Special Edition and
colophon are registered trademarks of the publisher.

America's Publisher of Contemporary Romance

Printed in the U.S.A.

BC91

Books by Patti Beckman

Silhouette Romance

Silhouette Special Edition

The Movie

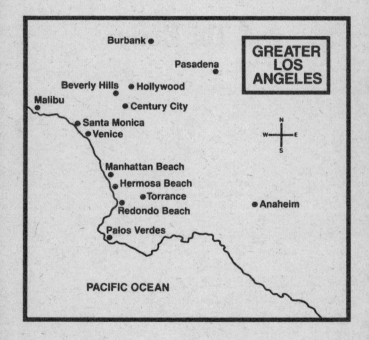

GREATER
LOS
ANGELES

Burbank ●

Pasadena ●

Beverly Hills ● ● Hollywood
Malibu ●
● Century City

● Santa Monica
● Venice

Manhattan Beach ●

Hermosa Beach ●
● Torrance
Redondo Beach ●

● Palos Verdes

● Anaheim

PACIFIC OCEAN

N
W ✦ E
S

Chapter One

*H*ollywood . . .

Natalie Brooks gazed over the smog-shrouded panorama of Los Angeles. From this dusty old office building window she could see the hills of Hollywood in the distance. The view brought a fresh edge to the pain within her. Hollywood—the symbol of make-believe, the shimmering fabric of dreams, of glittering fantasies. She knew that aspect well. She was a part of it. But her own life drama was not pretend. Her heartache was not emotion simulated before a camera lens. It was very deep, very private and very real.

Then she realized her agent, Ira Bevans, was speaking to her. With an effort, she controlled her wandering attention and turned. Her gaze swept the cluttered office. It was a large, old-fashioned room in an outdated building. A half century's refuse from the movie industry was stacked around in piles and pasted on the walls. There were framed pictures of Harlow, Gable, Garbo, Bogart alongside faded photographs of Cecil B. De Mille, Jack L. Warner, Louis B. Mayer. Ira Bevans was in many of the pictures, either with an arm around or shaking hands with a celebrity. Each was autographed, "To my good friend, Ira . . . I love you, Ira. . . ."

The air was musty. Stacks of old contracts that long ago should have been discarded contained the details of client studio deals going back to the silent movie days.

"I'm sorry, Ira. You were saying?"

The man seated behind a wide expanse of a mahogany desk leaned back, stroking his shiny scalp, and gazed at her thoughtfully. Ira was a small man, thin and dry as parchment. Out of the wrinkled, leathery texture of his face glittered a pair of brown eyes still reflecting as much kinetic energy as had gone into negotiations with Louis B. Mayer's MGM studios.

"I was discussing the talk shows, sugar. Remember *Never Tomorrow?* The movie being released this week? You're the star. Or maybe you forgot already?"

She blushed. "You don't have to be sarcastic, Ira."

"Sarcastic? What sarcastic? I'm concerned, sugar. You're off in another world. You haven't heard two words since you came in here this morning. You're walking around this office like a lion in a cage."

Natalie sighed. She tried to control her restlessness by taking a seat in one of the comfortable old plush office chairs facing Ira's enormous desk. She toyed with the thought that perhaps Jean Harlow or Carole

Lombard might have once sat in this same chair facing this same desk. She crossed sleek, long legs. "I apologize, Ira. You have my undivided attention."

Her agent scrutinized her with a penetrating gaze that made her uncomfortable. Ira was one of those few people in the world who knew the real Natalie Brooks. He knew as much about her private life as anyone alive. More, she sometimes thought with a tinge of resentment, than he should. She loved Ira, but he could be extremely nosy. He was of the old-school Hollywood agents who put their agent-client relationships on a very personal basis. Still, she had no real complaints. Ira had negotiated some fabulous movie and TV deals for her.

Standing five feet five and weighing all of a hundred pounds dripping wet, Ira Bevans gave the impression of an angry sparrow about to pounce on an offending worm. His scorn for some contemporary male Holly-wood dress modes involving sport shirts open to the navel and pendants dangling from gold chains was vitriolic. He would refuse to be caught dead in anything but one of his tailor-made suits, imported shirts and ties. He stopped on the way to the office every morning to have his shoes polished to a mirror shine. His jewelry consisted of a diamond stickpin, an expensive watch and a large diamond ring on the small finger of his right hand.

Ira had once been one of the great agents around town. His cronies included some of the most powerful movie and TV producers, actors and studio heads as well as the unseen powers that ran the industry, the advertising agencies and corporate executives. With the demise of the old studio system, the passing of the

Hollywood moguls and the shift of power in the industry to the corporate boardrooms in New York, Ira's fortunes had been on the decline. He seemed destined to join the memorabilia in his office, the musty contracts and faded photographs of another era. But then, by a stroke of good fortune, he had handled Natalie Brooks's first acting contract. Her meteoric rise to stardom in a few short years had put Ira back in the mainstream, which to an old man living as much in the past as in the present was like taking a bath in the fountain of youth. The corporate lawyers sent around to deal with Ira had approached the old man with a condescending air, only to find themselves crossing swords with a mind as sharp as surgical steel and quick as a darting rapier. The result had been contracts that made Natalie one of the highest-paid stars of the year and put Ira back into a tax bracket that both awed him and made him furious with the Internal Revenue Service.

Now he settled forward and rustled some papers on his desk. "The talk shows," he repeated. "We've lined up guest appearances for you with Johnny Carson, and next week you're supposed to fly to New York to do 'Good Morning America.' That will coincide with the premier of *Never Tomorrow.* . . ."

His voice trailed away. He put his cigar in an ashtray and shoved the papers aside. He leaned back, his bright brown eyes narrowed. "You're not listening again."

Natalie felt her cheeks grow warm. "Yes, I am. Johnny Carson, 'Good Morning America.' I heard."

"You can fly to New York next week?"

"Yes, yes, yes!"

"Now you're getting snippy with poor old Ira." His voice took on a hurt tone. "Poor old Ira who loves you like his own daughter and just wants the best for his little girl."

Tears glinted in her eyes. "Ira, I'm sorry. I—I guess I'm on edge today. Forgive me."

"Forgive? What's to forgive?" He rose with a sigh, came around the desk to pat her shoulder awkwardly, then moved to the window, taking in the same view that had absorbed her moments ago. "I know what it is, sugar. Old Ira knows. It's that schlemiel, Kirk Trammer. He's back in the States. I heard all about it."

"He's no schlemiel, Ira."

"No? How can you say that after the way he treated you, sugar?"

There was a moment's silence while Natalie wondered at the way she had instinctively leaped to Kirk's defense. What was the matter with her, anyway? She had to be soft in the head. Kirk Trammer deserved every name Ira could think up to call him, and more!

"Yeah, I heard all about it," Ira went on bitterly. "Kirk Trammer, the great director. God's gift to the movies. Back from his little artsy, European avant-garde films—they don't call them movies over there; they call them 'films'—and now he's going to do this great blockbuster that'll turn Hollywood around. The trouble is, there ain't a studio on the West Coast that will touch him with a ten-foot pole."

"You shouldn't be so hard on him, Ira." Then Natalie thought, *There I go again, standing up for Kirk*. Was it going to be this way for the rest of her life?

Ira turned from the window. "Oh, sugar, I haven't got a thing against Kirk personally. So, maybe he is a genius like some critics think. Another Orson Welles or George Lucas, some of them say. What do I know about geniuses? All I got against Kirk is the way he treated you."

Natalie fought a sudden rush of tears. The last thing she needed right now was Ira's sympathy. It was taking all her effort not to break down.

But Ira was off on one of his tirades and nothing was going to slow him down. "All those articles in the fan magazines, the cheap grocery store tabloids, the big shiny slick publications, each with their own 'Untold Story' about Natalie Brooks, about her private life, about her love affairs.

"You want to know what they are out there, sugar? Cannibals, that's what. They sit around in their dull little lives hungry for gossip like a drug addict for a fix. The media turns a nice girl into the current sex queen and it starts, the myths, the lies. Once it was Jean Harlow, then Marilyn Monroe. Only day before yesterday it was Farrah, and yesterday Bo Derek and today it's Natalie Brooks. Minute-by-minute details about how Harlow died. Did Marilyn Monroe really kill herself? The gossip headlines give them all the emotions lacking in their own empty lives; the public wants to wallow in pity, shock, scorn, envy, love and hate. They want all the titillating details about who the sex queen is sleeping with; and if she ain't sleeping with anybody, the gossip makers, the press agents, the writers, the media will put somebody in her bed.

"Most of the time there's not a word of truth in any of it! So what? The truth doesn't sell newspapers or satisfy gossips. How disappointed those vultures out there would be if they knew the truth about Natalie Brooks, that she doesn't live on an exotic diet of herbs and natural foods to keep her incredible figure so slim, her complexion so flawless. She doesn't have a string of lovers. Natalie Brooks is truthfully a straight-forward, unselfish girl who is a soft touch for anybody in trouble. She doesn't take drugs or smoke pot. She doesn't even smoke cigarettes. Sex Goddess? Ha! Look at you right now. Dressed casually. Very little makeup. Still a lady down to the tips of your toes. Everything about you spells class—the way you pro-nounce every word so perfectly, the poise, the good manners, the aristocratic breeding. Another Grace Kelly. The only thing the gossips got right is that smartass Kirk leaving you to go sulking off to Europe because his big feature motion picture bombed out. That they got right, except for the lies they told about you. For that, I could kill all of them!"

"Ira, for heaven's sake, you're getting your ulcer all stirred up. Calm down, will you? That's all in the past. Kirk is in the past. It doesn't bother me anymore."

"Oh, it doesn't? I guess maybe what's on your mind is if the Dallas Cowboys are going to beat the Houston Oilers? Don't lie to old Ira. I saw it all over your face the minute you walked into the office this morning. You're all torn up over him being back in the States. Why didn't you divorce him while he was gone, anyway? Wash your hands of the bum! You're right. My ulcer is hurting." He opened a paneled cabinet, took out a packet of antacid powder, emptied it into a glass of water and gulped it down.

Feeling a sudden wave of concern, Natalie jumped

up and impulsively put her arm around her agent. "Please don't get yourself so worked up over me, Ira, honey. You shouldn't become so personally involved with your clients. I'm a big girl now, I can take care of myself."

"I'm not so sure," Ira muttered. "I can't help worrying about you, Natalie. You're too good-hearted. You're a patsy. In this business, you got to learn to be tough. Sometimes your best friends are your worst enemies, like that bunch you started hanging around with when you went to USC. The new breed of moviemakers. They're going to change the industry. The young rebels they call themselves, the Lucases, Coppolas, Spielbergs and Kirk Trammers. Sure, the industry has changed. The great old moguls like the Goldwyns, the Zanucks are gone. Now the studios are owned by the big corporations out East. But it's still the studios that run the show, put up the money, control the distribution, and don't you forget it."

"Why on earth are you telling me all that stuff, Ira? What has that got to do with my personal life?"

"Just a word of warning, honey, from a guy old enough to be your grandfather who's lived and breathed this business for fifty years. You're a star, Natalie. You're big box office. You got a fabulous future ahead of you. I worry that Kirk Trammer and that crazy bunch of USC friends of yours are going to get you involved in something you'll regret. You're too big for that now. You outgrew your friends. Maybe that sounds cruel, but it's true, and in this business you got to look out for number one, or they'll eat you alive."

Natalie frowned, eyebrows drawing pensively over huge brown eyes. Did Ira know something he wasn't telling her, or was he second-guessing? He claimed to have ESP where the Hollywood scene was concerned. Nevertheless, she felt something of a shock that he would mention her USC friends. Was it just coincidental that she had been invited for a get-together of the old crowd over at Bill and Sally Dentmen's Malibu beach house tonight? There was no way Ira could know about that, or could he? Why was he tying this all in with his tirade about Kirk? She knew Ira had never liked Kirk, so she wasn't surprised that he would become all stirred up over Kirk's return to the States. But she sensed something else was in the wind, something that made her vaguely uneasy beyond the natural emotional turmoil Kirk's return had awakened.

With one of his sudden changes of mood, Ira dropped the subject of her personal life and became all business. For the next fifteen minutes, he explained the intricacies of the various contracts and financial statements on his desk that required her signature.

With that out of the way, Natalie left his office and took the elevator to the parking garage where her bright red Porsche was waiting. A few minutes later, she was pulling away from the building into the flow of Los Angeles traffic.

She felt detached from the traffic around her, the sound of horns, the swish of tires on pavement, the rumble of engines. Automatic reflexes took over her handling of the powerful little car. Her mind was saturated with painful memories; the image of intense, hazel eyes, waving hair carelessly combed, a mouth that could be sensitive or angry, broad shoulders, strong arms. The nights of romantic fulfillment she had known in those arms woke remembered waves of heat coursing through her body and stabbed her heart with pain.

She might try to hide her feelings from Ira but she couldn't hide them from herself. Fortunately, she wasn't involved in shooting a movie at the present time; in her state of mind she'd never be able to remember her lines.

Pushing sentiment aside, she thought with a wave of anger that Ira was right. What she needed to do was settle this matter once and for all. She was never going to have any peace by clinging to those good times she and Kirk had shared. They were long gone. Kirk had by now no doubt forgotten them. She was a sentimental idiot to brood over something that was ended. She supposed she would always love Kirk, but she had her own life and career to think about, as Ira had wisely pointed out.

She raised her chin with a gesture of defiance and determination. Sooner or later, she was going to have to have a confrontation with Kirk. She would tell him she wanted to get the matter of the divorce settled.

She left the Ventura Freeway, merging with the southeast-bound traffic on the Hollywood Freeway. She was driving through familiar territory. Here, in roughly a fifty-square-mile area were situated the studios, the sound stages, the lots, all the facilities of the movie industry. In the northern section were the Disney, Universal and Burbank studios. At the southern tip was MGM and United Artists studios on the Metro-Goldwyn-Mayer lot. To the east were Paramount Pictures and the ABC studios, and to the west, Twentieth Century-Fox.

This was the place the world knew as Hollywood, where artists wove the tapestry of imagination and fantasy on movie and TV screens to satisfy the dreams of the world.

She passed landmarks like the John Anson Ford Theater and the Hollywood Bowl. She took an exit and saw the street signs of Sunset, Vine and then Santa Monica Boulevard, that would take her to her home in Beverly Hills.

On the way, she turned off at Rodeo Drive, that cluster of exclusive shops, boutiques, cafés and banks contained in a few blocks of glittering opulence. Names like Cartier, Van Cleef and Arpels, Gucci lined the street. It was the shopping center for movie stars and millionaires, an area that ranked with Paris's Faubourg St. Honoré, London's Bond Street and Rome's Via Condotti. Rolls-Royces, Lincolns and Mercedes filled the parking areas. In the shops one could spend as much as $24,000 for a topcoat or $38,000 for a bedspread. It was a street where famous stars rubbed elbows with oil rich sheiks from Saudi Arabia or corporate executives from New York.

Natalie strolled through Rodeo Drive's newest mall, the Rodeo Collection. It was a three-story structure with more than thirty-five stores including glorious art galleries and specialized elegant boutiques. There was Portuguese marble construction with lots of glass and bronze trim and various walls of hand-laid bricks in intricate patterns. From the penthouse level huge pots of white jasmine floated down the cascading glass windows to the lower level. It was a glittering fairyland of exotic plants, solid brass rails costing $450 a running foot and a scenic glass elevator. The mall housed such couture shops as Fendi, Nina Ricci, Ungaro and Luis Vuitton.

The same restlessness churned in her that had made her so jumpy in Ira's office. The minutes of an emotional time bomb were ticking away inside her. She couldn't get her mind off the matter of Kirk's being back in California and the fact that, sooner or later, she was going to encounter him face-to-face. That prospect was like a gathering storm on the horizon, threatening to rip her life asunder again. That was the effect Kirk always had on her existence. Her nerves were drawn tight.

Natalie was in a strange, reckless mood. After a champagne and caviar lunch at Nipper's, she was seized with the impulse to buy something casual yet wildly extravagant for the Malibu beach party tonight. At one of the designer shops, she found just what she was looking for—a beach ensemble that consisted of a flowered wraparound top and sarong which, untied, cleverly revealed a hidden bikini. It was exactly the kind of abandoned, daring statement she wanted to make. She signed a check for eight hundred dollars. The clerk accepted it without hesitation. Everyone in the store had recognized her. They waited on movie stars every day. Still, Natalie's beauty and current popularity made her something of a VIP among celebrities.

She left the store, putting on sunglasses to shield her eyes from the bright California sunshine. On her way to her car she was stopped several times by fans eagerly requesting her autograph. She complied, smiling, wondering if these strangers had any inkling of the emotional turmoil boiling inside the person they saw as a poised, glamorous movie star. Today she was much more aware of her role in real life as a woman confronted by heartbreak.

Then she was in her car, speeding to the home she had once shared with Kirk. It was one of those huge old Spanish-style homes built in the 1920s in the heyday of the great silent movie stars who drank bootleg gin from sterling silver pocket flasks and drove around in enormous twelve-cylinder Packards. The great stucco-and-tile structures were built in the canyons and hills that had once been the territory of deer and coyotes. Originally built by a 1920s queen of the silent screen, the home had been owned by a series of famous stars through the thirties and forties to the present. It had enormous fireplaces, great, rough-hewn beams and stained-glass windows. There was an imposing winding stairway. Natalie imagined that the silent movie vamp had specially designed it so she could sweep down it for a dramatic entrance to welcome her glamorous guests.

The place had fallen into disrepair by the time Kirk and Natalie took it on. The swimming pool was cracked; all the plumbing was clogged with rust and had to be ripped out and replaced. The disintegrating tennis court was growing a crop of weeds and grass. They had spent a small fortune restoring the place. Kirk had delighted in turning one of the great rooms (Natalie called them chambers) into a private theater viewing room fitted with the latest projection equipment.

Concerned with security as were most stars these

days, Natalie had the place surrounded with a chain link fence with an electronically controlled gate blocking the winding driveway.

Natalie had never been very enthusiastic about the house. She had secretly thought of it as something of a Gothic monstrosity. But she had kept her feelings to herself because Kirk liked it. After Kirk went off to Europe, she grew to hate this place. It had become a cold, empty castle. Now she wanted to dispose of it. She thought as soon as they agreed on a divorce and property settlement she would either move into a place like Bill and Sally Dentmen owned on the beach or she would find a secluded little ranch in one of the beach canyons like Topanga where she could raise dogs and horses.

When she was on the East Coast, she either stayed at her mother's palatial home in Tuxedo Park on the Hudson or in the apartment she kept in Manhattan. But when she was in Hollywood, for reasons she couldn't entirely define, she continued to make this big old house her home. Perhaps it was because the memories of the brief happiness she had shared with Kirk lingered within these walls. When she curled up under the covers of the king-size bed, she felt close to the nights Kirk had lain beside her, drawing her into his arms. It was as if their lovemaking had imbued the satin sheets with a warmth that lingered on long after the whispered words of love and passion had been stilled.

Unwanted memories stole through her being, awakening hungers and needs that she tried to forget. Her body would ache with longing for the intimate caress of Kirk's touch; the heat that came in mounting waves coursing through her as his kisses set her aflame; the throbbing desire that he alone could arouse; the fulfillment and satisfaction that their love-making could bring. The bittersweet memories tore at her throat with unbearable pain and drenched her pillow with tears.

She both hated and loved the house for those memories of her and Kirk together—memories that haunted the place long after Kirk was gone and their love story had ended.

She parked her sports car in the spacious garage. On the way to the house, she waved to her gardener, Kim Yusota, who was trimming a hedge. Kim and her live-in housekeeper, Maria Alequestra, were all the staff Natalie kept here now.

There had been a larger staff when she and Kirk were living together. Kirk was gregarious. The big old house had been alive with parties and throngs of friends. Kirk was one of those multitalented individuals. Moviemaking was his all-consuming passion, but he was also a skillful amateur magician and a jazz musician. Sometimes he and his musician buddies would hold all-night jam sessions in the music room. It had been exciting, living with Kirk, Natalie thought, and then, catching herself slipping into painful reminiscing, she resolutely put those thoughts out of her mind.

In the house, she explained to the housekeeper that she would not be having her evening meal at home because she was driving out later to spend the night with friends at Malibu.

She changed into a swimsuit and went down to the pool for a dip. She swam hard for several laps around the Olympic-size pool, finding some relief from her emotional tension by exhausting herself physically. Then she stretched out on a towel, drenching her body in the golden sunshine.

Half-dozing, her mind wandered, drifting through a montage of memories. Like a spectator watching a movie flickering across the silver screen, she felt detached, seeing glimpses of the events that had shaped events and brought her to this point in her life. Was there really any such thing as free will, she wondered. Had she had any control over the times, good and bad, that had made her what she was now? Looking back, she thought it was as if a giant, unseen hand of fate had moved her about like a pawn in a great game whose meaning was beyond her grasp.

She could have been born into a family of refugees in the strife-torn Middle East, or the child of a blue-collar worker in the South, or the daughter of migrant farm parents. But fate had started her life in the home of a socially prominent mother and father who divided their time between their estate on the Hudson and their summer place in Southampton, New York. Her mother was a respected actress in New York theater circles. Her father was a senator. She had dim, childhood memories of a tall, dashing man who tossed her in the air, called her his princess and spoiled her with toys. But she had hardly begun to know him before a car wreck took him away forever. Her mother told her he was in heaven watching over her, but that hadn't satisfied a young girl's hunger for a real daddy. She often dreamed of having a father like her friends had, and she'd wake up with tears on her pillow.

Her mother, an ageless beauty, had a lengthy string of suitors. She had loved Natalie's father, but she was too much of a social butterfly to spend the rest of her life grieving. She filled her days with her community and social activities. Natalie spent the winters in private, fashionable boarding schools, coming home for vacations. Her mother's stately home was the setting for endless social events, charity fund-raising campaigns and parties.

The sunlight on Natalie's body turned cold and her thoughts grew dark as she remembered the year she was twelve. Home from boarding school for the summer, she was introduced to her mother's suitor, a big, swarthy man who owned a fleet of merchant ships.

The man, Olan Koener, was to become her stepfather. She had disliked him from the first day she set eyes on him. He was a hard, cold man who had no concept of how to relate to children. With her mother, he was tender and courteous. But to Natalie, he was a dictator. Although he had never actually abused her, she was afraid of him. There was a look of cold steel in his eyes that terrified her. The atmosphere in the house was strained when she was home. He always looked relieved when she left for boarding school.

Her unhappy relationship with her stepfather began a pattern of making her a withdrawn and lonely little girl. The situation was made worse by her childhood allergy attacks that bordered on asthma. Her stepfather, a robust man of Norwegian seaman stock, had little patience with illness. He accused her of malingering.

That was the beginning of the nightmares, the

drawing inside herself, the phobias. Her mother had been distraught, not knowing how to deal with an emotionally ill child. Natalie could not talk with her mother about her problems. They had never been close, and there are things a child cannot put into words. Eventually, there had been the year in the private hospital, the kind doctor who talked with her every day, until she was able to express the inner thoughts and fears that had made her sick. And then there had been a long, slow convalescence.

The doctor thought a change would be helpful. Natalie was sent out to California for a visit in the home of her mother's brother, Bill Wells, who lived in Hollywood. He was a highly skilled specialist in the field of creating special effects for movies. Natalie was terrified of men, but she gradually relaxed around her big, jolly uncle. And his daughter, Ginny, Natalie's cousin, became as close to Natalie as a sister. After that, Natalie looked forward to her yearly California visits.

During those adolescent years, while the acute stage of her emotional illness had improved, she had remained painfully shy, at a loss for words and unsure of herself, unable to cope with social interaction. In her school she was known as a loner. Some thought she was too stuck-up to make friends. That was totally wrong. She was desperately lonely. Then, she had stumbled on a magic cape she could wear that shielded her so she could shed her inhibitions and face the world. She tried out for a school play and got the lead role. On stage, she took on the personality of the part she was playing. Secure in that masquerade, she could give vent to all her emotions. It was all right to laugh out loud, to cry, to shout, to act funny or sad, because it wasn't Natalie Brooks doing those things; it was the story character she was playing.

The drama coach in her private school was enthralled. Here was natural acting talent such as she had not seen in a long time. Knowing nothing about the trauma that had left Natalie emotionally scarred, she attributed Natalie's ability to inheriting the talent from her actress mother, who was naturally flattered and delighted.

Natalie was developing into a raving beauty. Her aristocratic family background and expensive private schools had given her a cool, reserved poise. With those looks and an outstanding acting talent, how could she fail? From then on, Natalie had the best coaching in drama money could buy. Her mother tried to direct her to the legitimate stage, but Natalie's exposure to the magic of Hollywood through her uncle Bill and her cousin Ginny had set her course for her. She would go to USC, learn all she could about moviemaking. It was there that Bill and Sally Dentmen and Linda Towers came into her life. They had all been students then, with a common goal—a career in the movie industry. Bill and Sally wanted to write movie scripts. Linda's field was editing. Ginny planned to follow in her father's footsteps and work in special effects. For the first time, Natalie was part of a close-knit group of friends. They took the place of a family she'd never had. Her real father was only a fragmentary childhood memory. Her mother was a beautiful, shimmering butterfly who flitted in and out of her life, always just out of reach. But Bill and Sally and Linda and Ginny were real people who hugged her and talked with her and loved her. Together, they shared the excitement of being young and intense about their careers.

Then Kirk Trammer had come into her life. But at that point, she abruptly disregarded her turn of thoughts. It was time to dress and leave for Malibu.

Located in the northwestern part of Los Angeles County, Malibu—with its beaches washed by the Pacific Ocean—is populated by affluent names from the entertainment world, rock stars, actors, studio executives, TV stars and writers. It has a laid-back, relaxed, resortlike atmosphere.

Natalie arrived at the Dentmens' beach house just as the sun was going down in one of those dramatic Pacific sunsets that splashed riots of vivid hues across the heavens. The air was clear, most of the smog and mist having been swept away by the Santa Ana winds. The Dentmen cottage faced a stretch of white, sandy beach. A high wall festooned with red bougainvillaea blossoms shielded the residence from the Pacific Coast Highway.

Natalie parked in the driveway. She heard voices around front on the deck that faced the beach. The aroma of charcoal-broiling steaks assailed her nostrils.

She walked around to the deck. She paused for a moment, taking in the scene, feeling a warm glow at the sight of her friends. Bill Dentmen, a tall, stringbean type with sparse sandy hair and heavy-rimmed glasses that gave him a studious look, was standing over the barbecue grill. He was probing steaks that had been marinated in bourbon and honey, according to his own secret recipe. His wife, Sally, blond, and cheerfully plump, was shouldering the screen door open as she emerged carrying a salad bowl in both hands. Linda Towers, dark, slender, intensely beautiful, was in one of the deck chairs, engrossed in what appeared to be a story synopsis. Natalie's cousin, Ginny Wells, carrot-topped, freckled, forever a teenager, was still in her bathing suit, sprawled comfortably in a redwood deck lounging chair, smearing ointment on her sunburn.

Ten years had passed since they had been together in their first year of college. All of them now had full-time careers in the hectic profession of moviemaking. Bill and Sally, who had married while still in college, had by now written a number of successful screenplays. Linda Towers was one of the top film editors in the business. Ginny had become her father's partner in his special effects work. Of the group, however, Natalie's star had risen the highest. She smiled, thinking of the multitude of friends she could have if she wished. There were an endless string of individuals eager to become camp followers. But Natalie had remained reclusive. She had never fitted into the Hollywood social scene. When she wasn't involved in a motion picture project, she preferred to spend her time on the East Coast. When she was out here, she was comfortable only with these four, her closest buddies, whom she considered family.

"Hi gang," she called gaily, mounting the steps to the deck.

There was a chorus of responding greetings. Ginny hopped up, giving her a hug, followed by Linda and Sally. Bill, wearing his barbecue apron, holding his long-pronged fork, waited his turn to give her a kiss.

"That's a darling outfit," Linda Towers exclaimed, viewing Natalie's halter-sarong ensemble.

"Yeah, I had an acute attack of shopping fever this afternoon," Natalie confessed.

"By the way, congratulations," Bill said. "The critics say *Never Tomorrow* is going to be one of the year's biggies."

Natalie made a face. "It's not going to be an Academy nomination if that's what you mean. I suppose it will make the studio a few million, though."

"That's the name of the game, isn't it?"

"You guys should have written the script. Some of those lines were so corny!"

They settled into the deck chairs, gossiping about the film that was being premiered this week; laughing over the anecdotes Natalie related about *Never Tomorrow,* the usual funny, insane, unpredictable incidents that invariably occurred in the shooting of a motion picture. "You won't believe this, but you know what a sissy Tim Lowery, the associate producer, is. Well, we were using this tame old lion for that one scene. The poor old moth-eaten thing probably doesn't have any teeth left. He just wanted to be left alone so he could sleep. Anyway, somebody forgot to fasten his cage door. Tim came on the set eating a bologna sandwich. The lion smelled it, nudged his cage door open and came sauntering up behind Tim. The lion let out a roar—probably from hunger pangs. Tim spun around, turned white as a sheet, let out one awful scream and fainted dead away. So help me, he was stretched out cold and the lion was standing there, licking his face. The animal trainer was laughing so hard he didn't have the strength to pull the lion off. One of the gaffers came over and hit the lion on the snoot with a rolled-up newspaper and he went slinking back to his cage."

The story convulsed Bill, who almost dropped his fork. After the laughter subsided, Sally served glasses of wine. Then Bill said, "Steaks are ready."

They ate the delicious barbecued steaks and salad on paper plates and drank wine and talked, but Natalie began to sense that something was out of sync. There were momentary strained gaps in the conversation followed immediately by talk and laughter that seemed to her just a little bit forced. Natalie couldn't understand what was happening. In all of her other dealings with people in her profession, the actors, directors, studio executives, there was the sense of everyone playing a calculated role, saying one thing while constantly measuring responses, testing responses, judging strengths and weaknesses, never letting one's guard down. But these were her dearest friends. This was one group of people with whom she could be herself, totally relaxed. But not tonight. Something was in the air. Her conversation earlier today with her agent, Ira Bevans, flashed through her mind. He'd been uptight about something. What had he said? "I worry that Kirk Trammer and that crazy bunch of USC friends of yours are going to get you involved in something you'll regret. . . ." What had he meant by that? Had he known something she didn't?

She noticed the material that Linda Towers had been reading, tucked between her side and the arm of the chair. "Is that a new screenplay Bill and Sally are going to do?" Natalie asked in one of the curious lulls in the conversation.

Linda flushed. "Not exactly." She fished it out. She hesitated for a moment, then said, "It's the story synopsis of the new movie Kirk wants to film, Natalie."

The conversation on the beach-house deck faded to silence. Natalie was conscious of the surf matching the suddenly heavy pounding of her heart. She glanced around and realized that she had become the center of attention. There appeared to be a great deal of interest in her reaction. She thought all of her friends were carefully measuring her response. Why? Now she was certain she had been invited here tonight for a definite reason. Some kind of intrigue was afoot.

"You've seen Kirk, then?" she asked, her mouth strangely dry.

"Yes," Linda replied, nodding.

"It's a terrific story, Natalie," Bill Dentmen said. "Kirk wants Sally and me to write the screenplay."

Suddenly, the self-conscious tension that had been such a strain all evening broke in a rush of enthusiasm from all sides.

"I'm going to be in charge of special effects and Linda is going to be the film editor," Ginger Wells exclaimed.

Sally joined in. "Natalie, remember when we were all in school together, we said one day we were going to form our own production company and do a big blockbuster movie together? Well, it looks as if this is going to be it!"

"The story has everything," Bill agreed, "international intrigue, suspense, fast pace, a great love story.

I don't know when I've been so excited about a story idea."

"And don't forget all the special effects I'll get to create," Ginger said.

"With Kirk directing, it can be the big motion picture of the year, as big as *Star Wars* or *E.T.*," Linda agreed.

Natalie felt a growing sense of unease. She remembered the warning earlier today from her agent, Ira. It was starting to make sense. Had Ira known about this? Had Kirk approached him? Or had he gotten the information through the Hollywood grapevine?

"Why are you all telling me this?" Natalie asked her friends suspiciously. "You know Kirk and I have broken up. I haven't even heard from the guy in two years. I have no interest in his production plans."

Bill looked embarrassed. "You knew he was back in the States, didn't you?"

"Yes, but I only heard it secondhand. He hasn't tried to contact me."

Again there was an embarrassed silence.

Her irrepressible cousin, Ginny, broke the silence with a bombshell. "Natalie, Kirk wants you to play the female lead."

Natalie was stunned. She sat immobilized in shocked silence. Now Ira's hinted warning was clear. Now she understood the undercurrent of tension here tonight. Her thoughts were in disarray; her emotions were spinning. Suddenly the only clear thought she had was the way her entire existence had been turned upside down that day Kirk Trammer had first walked into her life. And now he was back, trying to do it all over again.

Chapter Two

$\mathscr{I}$t all came back in a rush, every fragment of memory since that first magic moment they met.

"Natalie, this is the fellow we've been telling you about, Kirk Trammer. Kirk, our good friend, Natalie Brooks."

The time, six years ago. The place, the campus of the University of Southern California, University Park, Los Angeles. Bill Dentmen had made the introduction.

There had been something disturbing, vaguely frightening about her first meeting with Kirk. At the time, Natalie blamed the uneasiness on her characteristic shyness that kept her reserved and self-conscious with strangers. Looking back, she now suspected it was a premonition that this man was going to change her life forever. A change that drastic could certainly be frightening.

He was tall, lanky, broad-shouldered, towering

over her own five feet seven. His hair was dark and bushy. His scuffed old Western boots, faded blue jeans and rumpled jacket indicated an impatience with, and indifference to, surface appearance.

There was something different about Kirk that instantly set him apart from the college bunch who had become her friends. He was older. His eyes were haunted with a firsthand knowledge of life and death and struggle that was not yet seen in the young men she met on the campus.

He had the most unusual eyes she had ever seen. They were large, slightly almond-shaped, framed with thick lashes. Her first impression was that they were of a translucent quality, glowing with dark, inner fires. Then she realized they were a light hazel, almost golden.

When she got to know him better and found out he had left home at sixteen; had searched the country from coast to coast on a motorcycle while working at odd jobs; had fought in Viet Nam; had carried a wounded buddy through a hail of sniper fire to a helicopter, for which he had received the bronze star; had come back to drive a truck; play piano with a jazz group; work in the oil fields; lose a girl he planned to marry—then she understood better those haunting eyes that gave him a maturity beyond his years.

She knew none of those things about him at their first meeting. She only knew that the touch of his hand made her body quiver and the sound of his voice did strange things to the tempo of her heart. This was no run-of-the-mill college boy she was meeting. This was a man with a driving purpose in life. And she sensed with a hot rush of blood to her cheeks that in his gaze moving over her there was a man's knowledge of a woman's body and he was measuring what he saw against that knowledge.

She was vaguely shocked at her own response to his searching, experienced gaze. Never had she so intensely felt her own womanhood. She felt her breasts suddenly full and aching, straining against her garments; her hips and waist, proudly asserting their curves; her thighs growing strangely warm, quivering slightly. She drew a shuddering breath, both frightened and aroused by the instant, overwhelming physical attraction.

Over the rushing torrent of her emotions she heard Bill Dentmen adding to the introduction, "Natalie, Kirk is the genius I told you about who has been shaking up all the professors in the school of cinema and television.

"Hardly a genius," Kirk shrugged, his dark eyes still directed toward Natalie as if at the moment she were the focal point of the universe.

"The heck you say," Bill said. "They don't know exactly what to make of you. You break all the rules and then come up with something spectacular."

Natalie barely heard the exchange. She was still struggling with the impact this man was making on her emotions and her senses. Some kind of chemistry was boiling that caused him to be instantly, overwhelmingly attractive. Was it the subtle masculine smells, the obvious strength and hardness of his physique under the jacket and the tight blue jeans that hugged his muscular thighs? Or was it that burning intensity in his dark eyes drawing her as a moth to the flame?

At that time, they were all in their last year at USC.

Kirk was involved in some graduate work. It was a world away from the life she had known back East, where she had grown up as a young socialite, a member of a prominent family, a debutante. When she had announced her decision to go to USC, her mother had not been pleased.

"Why go all the way to California? There are excellent colleges in New York," her mother had argued.

But Natalie was already packing. "Mother, I've checked into it. There are three schools in the country that have an outstanding film program: the University of California at Los Angeles, New York University and the University of Southern California. I've decided on USC."

"For the life of me, I can't see why you're so concerned about going to a school with a film-making curriculum. You're an actress. You could have a brilliant future on the stage. You're not going to be a cinematographer, for heaven's sake!"

"I know that. But it just seems that going to a school that has a film-making department will put me in closer touch with Hollywood. I can go to USC and enroll in their drama department and still take some cinema courses to learn something about movie-making. I've read that eighty percent of their graduates get into professional work somewhere in the film industry."

Her mother sighed. "Hollywood! With your talent you ought to be thinking about the stage."

"Perhaps. I'm not really sure what I want to do at the moment. At any rate, the stage hasn't exactly been beating down the door to get at me."

"If you'd let me, I could make a few phone calls. It might be just small walk-on parts at first but then—"

Natalie shook her head. She rarely disagreed with her mother, but this was a turning point in her life and she stood her ground. "It's not going to hurt my career to spend a few years in a big university until I decide what I'm going to do."

More than that, she thought, it was her declaration of independence from her mother and from the East Coast life imposed on her. For that reason she had decided on a college in Los Angeles, on the other side of the continent. She had enrolled in the school of performing arts at USC. Her decision had been made when she learned her cousin, Ginny Wells, was going to USC.

In the Cinema and Television Department, her cousin took courses like Techniques in Motion Picture Production, Motion Picture Camera, Film History and Criticism, Advanced Camera and Lighting, Motion Picture Processing and Motion Picture Sound Recording. In the drama department, Natalie enrolled in such courses as Stage Direction, Acting I and II, Acting for the Media II, Advanced Acting, Drama Performance and some experimental workshops. At the same time, she audited some of the cinema classes with Ginny.

It was through Ginny that Natalie got to know the ambitious young film makers in the school. It was an exciting time. She was surrounded by young people fired with the magic of cinema production. When not in class, they were staring at movie screens. Then they talked the evenings away over what they had seen, criticizing, dissecting, analyzing how the films were directed, the camera angles, the special effects, the script, the acting.

They made a pact. "One day, we'll form our own production company," Ginny exclaimed. "Bill and Sally will write the scripts. I'll do the special effects. Linda will handle the editing. And Natalie will be the star."

It was an agreement and a promise, made and accepted with assurance. They all felt that they had been touched by fate and one day it would all certainly come true.

Then Kirk exploded on the scene.

That fateful day when Bill introduced Natalie to Kirk, he explained, "Kirk is taking a graduate-level course, a workshop. During the semester, he has to make two fifteen-minute movies. He's rounding up some people for his film crew."

"Yes, and I need to find someone from the drama department to appear in a scene," Kirk added, still holding Natalie within the hypnotic confines of his gaze. "Could you find the time to help us? Would you be interested? It would only take one day."

"Well . . . I—I don't know," Natalie stammered, too flustered by his dynamic presence, and too startled by his request to think rationally. "Why me?"

"I saw you in the experimental theater workshop play last week. I was impressed."

"You were?" she asked, feeling awkward and painfully self-conscious. She wasn't on a stage now, hiding safely in a pretend role. This was reality, the kind she had so much difficulty handling. The raw emotions

Kirk Trammer had awakened in her were frightening. Her breathing felt strained. Standing close to him, she was acutely aware of so many things, the warmth of his body, the sunlight on his tanned face, the curve of his lips, the resonance of his voice. It was as if all her senses had suddenly become fine tuned. The sounds, sights and smells of the campus blended into a background blur as her attention was riveted on the man before her.

"Yes," Kirk said, "you have real acting talent. And in addition, you are exceptionally beautiful. You have a kind of regal beauty—cool, poised, elegant. You remind me of Grace Kelly. Once an audience sees you they won't forget you."

His words didn't sound like flattery. It was more like an objective, professional opinion. He spoke with an air of assurance and authority. She didn't know when she had encountered such self-assurance in a student.

She didn't know how to respond. To be told she was beautiful by such a vital and attractive man was thrilling even if it was not voiced in a personal manner. There was a moment of self-conscious silence, interrupted by Kirk, who asked impatiently, "Well, how about it, Miss Brooks? Do you want to be in our film?"

Natalie swallowed hard. She wasn't certain what she was getting into. She glanced at Bill Dentmen, who nodded encouragement. "Well . . . all right." She nodded. "Yes."

"Okay, fine," he said, smiling briefly. "We're going to pack the equipment into my station wagon today and drive out into the desert in the morning. Can you be ready to leave about three in the morning?"

"Three in the morning?" Natalie repeated weakly.

"Yeah, I want to have the camera set up to catch the sunrise."

"Do I have some lines to learn?"

"Don't worry about that. You won't have much to say, if anything. This is going to be a visual film; very little dialogue."

At three the next morning, in the pitch dark except for a canopy of stars, Natalie found herself crammed into an ancient, rusty station wagon overloaded with equipment and people. The crew consisted of five students besides herself, who bore the titles of writer-director, cameraman, editor, sound man and production manager. Obviously, she was the entire cast. She sat next to Kirk, who drove. On her other side was the cameraman, Toby Calkins, an overweight, bearded fellow in a cotton T-shirt, who settled into the car and immediately went to sleep.

No one had much to say. On the long, bouncing ride, jammed between the two men in the front seat, Natalie couldn't escape the touch of Kirk's body. At every turn his hard, muscular thigh pressed firmly against hers, sending a warm surge of blood through her body. Once, as he navigated a turn, his elbow brushed against her breast, causing her heart to lurch.

Where he had touched her, her breast suddenly ached and throbbed. A torment of mingled emotions clutched at her throat. She found this physical contact with him exciting in a way that was unnerving. Never before had she experienced the kind of sensations that raced over her nerve ends, causing them to tingle. She felt both disturbed and aroused. She couldn't remember feeling so acutely alive to every sensation, every emotion.

When they reached the location in a deserted strip of desert, Kirk leaped out and galvanized the crew into action with fast, precise orders.

For nearly two hours, Natalie sat in the station wagon, watching as Kirk ran the cameraman ragged, shooting footage of the rising sun, the landscape, the cactus.

The production manager had followed them in a vintage car, a 1930 Model A Ford coupe. Where they had located the ancient vehicle, Natalie couldn't begin to imagine. Later, she found out Kirk had talked a buddy into borrowing it from his father's classic car museum.

"Kirk wants you to wear this," the production manager said, bringing a dress around to the station wagon.

Natalie stared at the garment. She looked around at the wide-open spaces surrounding them. "Where am I supposed to change?" she demanded.

The production manager shrugged. "Here in the car, I guess. Nobody will see you. We're all busy over there where they're doing the shooting."

He left her with the dress which, when she gave it a closer look, turned out to be a faded evening gown of about the same vintage as the old car.

Natalie went through a series of awkward gyrations, changing from her shirt and jeans into the flowing garment in the front seat of the station wagon. She had brought along her makeup kit and did the best she could with her hair and face under the circumstances. She gasped when Kirk suddenly appeared at the window. Hastily, she pulled the dress down, covering her legs. With a flush, she wondered how much he had seen.

"All ready?"

"Yes."

They had parked the Model A Ford beside a clump of cacti. Kirk directed Natalie to get out of the vintage car, stand beside it for a moment, looking around, then walk directly toward the camera.

She stumbled around the barren soil in evening slippers, perspiring as the sun grew hotter, and they made take after take. She was beginning to suspect that the entire crew, especially Kirk, were completely insane. Nothing they were doing made any sense to her. When she tried to get Kirk to explain, he only shrugged impatiently. He was in the grip of some kind of concentrated, burning inner energy.

At one point, the production manager dragged a large wind fan and portable generator out of the back of the station wagon. He cranked up the generator. As it spluttered into life, the blades of the fan began turning, whipping up a cloud of dust. The wind tore at Natalie's hair and pasted the thin evening gown to every curve of her body. She was blinded by the flying dust. Over the roar of the fan and generator, she heard Kirk shouting instructions to her and the cameraman. She took several steps toward the camera. Suddenly, she lost her footing. A cry of despair was wrenched from her as she teetered blindly, waving her arms in a futile attempt to regain her balance, and then sprawled backward in the dirt. A flash of pain raced down her leg.

Somebody turned the fan off. Sobbing with pain and humiliation, still half-blinded by the dust, Natalie could barely make out the faces of the film crew in a circle around her, staring down at her. Their expressions registered numbed shock.

Kirk shouldered his way through the circle. He bent and scooped Natalie out of the dirt. She seemed light as a feather in his strong arms. He helped her to a standing position. "Are you all right?" he asked, surveying the damage. Then he muttered an expletive. "You must have fallen into a cactus bed. There's a prickly pear leaf stuck to your thigh."

Natalie could only cry helplessly.

"Hold on," Kirk muttered. "This is going to hurt." Gingerly, he grasped the cactus. He winced sympathetically as he pried it loose. Natalie gasped and gave vent to a fresh flood of tears.

"Okay, fellas," Kirk said to the others. "That's all the shooting for today. Let's get back to town."

Gently, he helped Natalie back to the station wagon. She cried out with pain as she tried to sit down. Kirk wadded up his jacket for her to sit on in a way that her injured thigh did not rest against the seat. He ordered the fat cameraman to ride home with the production manager so Natalie wouldn't be crowded in the front seat.

She caught a glimpse of herself in the rearview mirror. Her hair was a tangled mess. Her face was a mask of dirt and dust streaked with tears. She wanted to die.

The deadly silence on the ride home was interrupted only by an occasional fresh sob from Natalie as a jolt awakened the pain in her throbbing body. She thought that when she got hold of Bill Dentmen, she was going to tell him his friend Kirk Trammer was dangerously insane and should be put away where he wouldn't be a threat to society. Whatever had made him attractive to her when they first met was totally lost in this nightmare of humiliation.

He dropped off the members of the crew from the back seat. Then as he made several turns, she became aware that they were headed away from the college campus area. "What are you doing?" she demanded. "My dorm is in the other direction."

"I don't live on campus," he explained.

"What's that got to do with me?" she asked sharply, all the anger and frustration of the day reaching a boiling point. "Take me home!"

"Sure, but not right away. I feel responsible for what happened. I can't just dump you in this condition. Do you know anything about cactus thorns?"

"Only that they hurt," she said, wincing as she touched her throbbing thigh.

"Where are you from?"

"The East Coast."

"Then I can assume this is the first time you have fallen into a bed of cactus?"

"Yes, and I hope my last!"

"Well, there are some things about cactus thorns you ought to know about. They have little barbs on the end like tiny fish hooks. When I yanked the prickly pear leaf off your leg, I'm sure some of the thorns broke off and stayed under the skin. They'll itch and fester and cause you all kinds of problems if you leave them there. We need to get them out right away."

Natalie felt new tears forming. She gritted her teeth, wishing she had never met Kirk Trammer.

He followed winding roads up into the hills north of Bel Air. Finally they pulled into the driveway of a big, ramshackle old frame house. "Come on," he said, helping her out of the station wagon. "Let's see if we can give you some first aid."

All of her will had drained out of her. Numbly, she allowed him to lead her into the house, limping as she walked. Her leg felt as if it were on fire.

He switched on the lights as they entered the hallway, then directed her into a large room off to the right. It appeared to be a kind of study or work room. The walls were covered with old movie posters and glossy stills. Papers and books were stacked everywhere. On one table was a Moviola—a film editing machine.

"I think it would be best for you to sit here," he said gently, leading her to a straight-back chair. As angry as she was with him, she couldn't help but appreciate the kind, gentle concern he was showing. Under normal circumstances, her shyness and uneasiness around men would have made her painfully uptight, being alone in this big old house with just Kirk. But he was treating her with the chivalry and tenderness of an older brother. And her pain and emotional exhaustion gave her a sense of detachment from reality. The day seemed so outrageous, it was like playing a part in some kind of ridiculous slapstick comedy.

When she was seated in the chair, he knelt beside

her. "Now if you don't mind, let's see how bad that leg is."

Natalie suddenly realized she was still wearing that ridiculous evening dress. It was in shambles, torn and covered with dust. Kirk lifted the hem, rolling it up above her knees.

The situation suddenly took on a sharp reality. Natalie felt a rush of blood to her cheeks as her long, sleek legs were bared. Her modesty was in shambles. She swallowed and her breathing felt strained. She forgot all about her pain in the acute awareness of Kirk, kneeling beside her, gazing at her uncovered thigh. But he was somehow maintaining an impersonal air, like a physician examining a wound.

"This may sting a little, but you'll feel better when we get those thorns out," he promised. He went off to a bathroom and came back with a pair of tweezers. He moved a floor lamp closer for better light. Again he knelt beside her. His left hand grasped her thigh, holding the area firmly as he began plucking out the thorns.

Her anger was dissolving in the warmth that spread from the touch of his hand all through her body like a soft, pulsating glow. Once again she had to deal with the effect his attractiveness had on her. She found it impossible to look at anything except his hands intimately touching her thigh as he carefully, gently removed the thorns. His fingers were long, like those of an artist, and had the strength of a craftsman. They were the kind of fingers that could hold a chisel as they carved an exquisite statue out of marble. The nails were kept short and clean. Dark hairs curled above the knuckles.

Her churning emotions fantasized those masculine hands taking more liberties, exploring her thighs with an intoxicating caress, finding delicate areas of heightened response, searching for a secret pocket of warmth that could set her entire body aflame. She felt both shocked and stimulated by the throbbing fantasies.

If there was pain involved in removing the thorns, she was no longer aware of it. She found such pleasure in his touch that she wanted the operation to go on indefinitely.

But after twenty minutes, he looked up, smiling. "Looks like we got all of them. Feel better?"

"Yes," she mumbled. Now, in a sudden, painful return of modesty, she covered her legs.

"I guess you'd like to get out of that costume," he said. "If you want to clean up and change, the bathroom is at the end of the hall."

He went out to the car and brought her the jeans and blouse she had worn to the desert location. In the bathroom, she stared aghast at her reflection in the mirror. The caked dust on her face had turned her into a caricature. She washed her hair and face, then spent the next half hour soaking in a tub of warm, soapy water. With a thick towel, she dried herself until her entire body was a glowing, tingling pink. She dressed in her jeans and blouse, checked the mirror and was pleased at what she now saw.

As she was leaving the bathroom, she became aware of a piano playing a familiar melody. Intrigued, she followed the sound to one of the spacious old rooms on the other side of the hall. She stood in the doorway, surprised to find Kirk at the keyboard of a battered upright. He was playing the old standard, "As Time Goes By."

Natalie leaned against the piano, watching his fingers move skillfully over the keyboard, impressed at how good he was. When he finished the romantic melody with a flourish, he looked up, smiling. Their eyes met. Natalie smiled. She said softly, "Play it again, Sam."

Kirk chuckled. "Bogart didn't really say that in *Casablanca,* you know."

"Yes," she nodded. "I know. But he should have."

Kirk rose. "Are you hungry?"

She suddenly realized she was famished.

He led her to the kitchen where he had arranged a platter of fruit, cheese, cold meats and wine.

With his courtly air, he pulled out a chair and seated her at the kitchen table. "Where did you learn to play the piano like that?" Natalie asked.

"The usual way. When I was a kid my parents made me take lessons. I hated practicing, but they made me keep at it. One day it dawned on me that I loved music. I've been grateful to my parents ever since. Now I pay part of my tuition expenses by playing with a jazz group on weekends."

"Did you grow up here in California?"

"No, Arizona. How about you?"

"The East Coast. Long Island."

"Umm." He gave her one of his analytical, measuring looks. "Rich family, expensive finishing school, right?"

She blushed self-consciously. "Is it that apparent?"

"Certainly. The diction. The poise. The good manners. The aristocratic bearing. The Grace Kelly look."

"You make me uncomfortable."

"Why? I don't mean to. I was just stating a fact. Most women would take it as a compliment."

"Yes, I suppose they would."

There was a comfortable silence as she tasted the cold fruit and had a sip of wine. It was an inexpensive domestic brand, but delicious. She lingered for a moment with the thought of how strangely relaxed she was with him now. She said, "You're quite a different person from when you were directing the filming out in the desert."

"Oh? In what way?"

"You're more human now. Out there . . . well, something seemed to be driving you."

"Yes, I suppose it was," he said thoughtfully. "Making motion pictures is my life now. You don't do anything well unless you lose yourself completely in it. You have to throw everything you have into it, forgetting everything else except the effect you're striving for. I intend to make some great motion pictures. You don't do that by playing at it. You have to be totally dedicated . . . committed."

She was riveted by the intensity in his eyes, fascinated by it, intrigued and a bit intimidated. She was not accustomed to such inflamed ambition. But then she thought that "ambition" was not a good description. She sensed more of a purpose, a mission almost amounting to zeal in his attitude. "Have—have you always felt this way?"

He laughed. "Lord, no. Until I went into the

military, I was just a kid out looking for a good time. I didn't give a thought to the future or what I wanted to do with my life. I just scraped through school with barely passing grades. I was a motion picture and TV junkie. Instead of doing my homework, I spent my time in movie theaters. One Christmas my folks gave me a movie camera. I turned the kids in the neighborhood into a production company. I spent all my allowance on film, making amateur home movies. But it was all just a game. I never considered seriously getting into the movie industry. I was having too much fun chasing around the country on my motorcycle. Then there was a hitch in the service . . . Viet Nam. When I came back, I was wilder than ever, trying to make up for the fun I'd been missing, I guess. Bought a brand new motorcycle, the most powerful on the market. One day I missed a turn, plowed into a tree. It was a bad wreck. A good friend riding with me was killed. . . ."

Natalie saw something wrench in his eyes like the twisting agony of a deep wound. He took a swallow of his wine. "Lying in the hospital with almost every bone in my body broken, I had a lot of time to do some thinking. For the first time, it dawned on me that I wasn't going to live forever and maybe there was more to life besides just having a good time. Sounds kind of corny now when I try to explain it. All I know was something inside me was changed from that moment on. Somehow it had become important for me to do something with my life . . . maybe it had something to do with my friend who had been killed. When I finally got out of the hospital, I had a purpose, a direction for my life. It was kind of like one of those born-again experiences some people talk about. I wanted to go back to school. What would I study? Well, why not the thing that had interested me the most when I was growing up? My head was filled with the images, the fantasies, the myths of the movies, the TV stories, the comic books that I'd saturated myself with as a kid. I couldn't think of anything I could put my whole self into except making movies." He shrugged with a wry smile. "So here I am."

Listening to Kirk, Natalie had lost all sense of time and place. His personality was overwhelming. She had no difficulty visualizing him taking command of a motion picture production company. As a director he would be a born commander, absolutely certain of where the film was going, listening to nothing except the creative voice within himself, seeing nothing except the vision in his own mind.

"Sorry if I've bored you, telling my life's story," he apologized. "I usually don't go on like this. Must be because you're such a good listener."

"I wasn't bored," she exclaimed truthfully.

His riveting gaze swept over her. "How about you, Natalie? What has motivated the aristocratic beauty of East Coast society to become an actress? I thought debutantes like you married foreign royalty or the presidents of giant corporations."

She felt a surge of anger. At times he had a talent for saying things that got under her skin. Was he doing it deliberately? "You seem to have put me into a convenient, shallow stereotype."

"Sorry. Didn't intend to insult you. I'm just curious about you."

She frowned, looking away. She couldn't explain to

him or anybody the shaping of her life that had turned her into an actress. It was too personal, too painful. "Acting just happens to be the only thing I'm any good at," she shrugged. Then her lips twisted in a wry smile. "I wouldn't be any good married to foreign royalty or the head of a corporation conglomerate."

"Touché." He nodded, a strange kind of light in his eyes flaring as he gazed at her. "From what I've seen of your acting, you'll have a bright career. You're one of the lucky ones."

"Lucky ones?"

"Yes . . . for some people, everything in life just falls into place effortlessly. Fate smiles on them."

She frowned, not sure of what he meant and uncertain of how to pursue the matter. She changed direction slightly. "I didn't have a chance to do much acting out there on the desert today! What on earth are you trying to do with that film, anyway?"

He waved a hand. "I'm sure it didn't make much sense to you. Wait until we have it edited. I won't try to explain until you see a finished cut."

A week later, on campus, she caught sight of his bushy dark hair and lanky frame. He waved and headed in her direction. He was in his usual attire, Western boots and rumpled jeans. He had shadows under his eyes and a two-days' growth of beard, the result of days and nights of intense editing work. "Hi. Just got our answer print. Would you like to see it?"

At first his words didn't register. Her thoughts were too involved with seeing him again. For the past week she had been able to think of very little except Kirk Trammer. Never had a man made such an impression on her. He had cost her a lot of sleepless nights. Over and over she had asked herself the ageless question—was there such a thing as love at first sight? When she closed her eyes, his image was burned in her memory. Her ears were filled with the sound of his voice. She remembered the texture of his skin, the masculine smells that surrounded him, the intensity of his gaze that made her knees weaken. In her reverie, she recalled every word they had spoken. When she remembered how tenderly he had picked her up and carried her, her heart melted. She thought of how he had treated the cactus wound and the flesh of her thigh burned with the memory of his touch. She had gone around in a daze, wondering if he would call, if she would ever see him again.

And now, here he was, inches away, drenching her senses again with his closeness, drowning her emotions in his gaze. With an effort, she shook off her hypnotic state. "I—I beg your pardon?"

"The answer print," he said. "I wondered if you'd like to come over to my place tonight to see it."

"Forgive me, but what's an answer print?"

"The first combined sound-and-picture print sent over to us from the lab for approval. You know, an approval print, a first-trial print."

"Oh, yes. The desert film. Of course I'd like to see it!"

"Great." He grinned enthusiastically. "I'll pick you up at your dorm about seven. Okay?"

Happily, she hugged her armful of books. "Yes . . . okay."

"How's the leg?"

Her face warmed at the memory of him bending

over her bared legs to treat the cactus wound. "It's much better," she stammered. "I guess you did the right thing, insisting on getting the thorns out."

He smiled, his hazel eyes gazing directly into hers, sapping the strength from her knees. He reached out and touched her cheek gently, sending a shiver through her body. "See you tonight, then. We'll stop off for hamburgers on the way."

Chapter Three

That night Natalie had found herself immersed in a crowd at Kirk's rambling old house. Besides the student production company that had worked on the assignment with him, there were more than a dozen other students from the university's cinema department, eager to see Kirk's newest film. Natalie's specially close friends, Bill, Sally, Linda and Ginny, were there. It was obvious to Natalie that, as Bill had said, Kirk was a legend on the campus. Word spread rapidly when he was making a film; everyone wanted to see his latest work. His student films had an originality and flair that set them entirely apart.

They gathered in Kirk's makeshift projection room, sitting in groups on the floor. Kirk operated the projector. From the moment the screen lit up, the audience was hypnotized. Natalie found her attention riveted on the screen. Her emotions were dazzled by the visual effects Kirk had created. It was a moving, impressionistic experience, achieved with startling camera angles, montages, slow and fast motion. In one segment, stop-frame photography produced a moving display of clouds roiling across the desert sky. When the scene merged into the one in which she was walking across the sand in the flowing evening gown suddenly caught in the man-made sand storm, she understood the effect of surprise and contrast Kirk had in mind. Now that day of madness on the desert made total sense. She felt respect for Kirk as a director who had known all along exactly what he was doing.

There was a moment of total silence when the film ended, followed by a burst of applause and excited conversation. For the next several hours, Kirk was in the center of an inspired group. Natalie felt isolated and somewhat out of place in this bunch of emerging moviemakers. She wandered around sipping a drink, wishing she could have Kirk to herself.

All the rooms on the ground floor of the old house had been converted into work areas. They were cluttered with books, papers, lighting and camera equipment. On one shelf, Natalie noticed a group of pictures of a strikingly beautiful young woman. In some of the pictures, the girl was with Kirk. One snapshot was a view of the two of them on a motorcycle. Several of the photographs were signed, "With love, Jacqueline."

Natalie felt a peculiar twinge. She hadn't considered the possibility that Kirk would be involved with someone. Now she was suddenly confronted with that situation and her emotions dipped in a cold lurch. Her feelings for Kirk were so new, so fragile, that she could not yet fully understand them herself. She wasn't prepared for the wrenching shock she experienced at the sight of another woman in Kirk's life, a woman who must be important to him or he wouldn't have this shrine of pictures. Where was she? There was no one in the crowd here tonight answering her description. Was she a girl back in his home town?

Her chaotic thoughts were interrupted as she was joined by Bill Dentmen. "What did you think of Kirk's film? It's really something else, isn't it?" he said enthusiastically. "Now maybe you'll believe me. The guy's a genius. You watch, Natalie. He's going to hit the movie industry like a bombshell."

"Yes," she nodded, trying to organize her thoughts. "You're a good friend of Kirk's, aren't you, Bill?"

"I don't know if you'd call me a good friend. I'm not sure if Kirk makes real close friends. He's something of a loner. But, I guess I'm as close to him as anyone on the campus."

She felt a cold uneasiness within. "I see he has a girl friend," Natalie murmured, nodding at the group of pictures. She was surprised at how directly she had posed the question. But she wouldn't have any peace until she knew the facts about Kirk and this young woman.

Bill glanced at the pictures and his gaze became somber. "Oh, yes. That's Jacqueline Davis. Hasn't he told you about her?" And he immediately answered his own question. "No, I guess he wouldn't. Jacqueline is a subject Kirk doesn't talk about."

"I don't understand."

"It was a tragedy in his life. Jacqueline was a young

rock singer on her way to becoming famous. They were engaged to be married. She was killed in an accident."

Suddenly Natalie remembered Kirk telling her about his motorcycle wreck. He had said a friend riding with him was killed, but he hadn't mentioned name or sex. He had just said "a friend." She recalled the glimpse of wrenching pain she had seen in his eyes, which he had quickly covered up. Now she understood a great deal more about Kirk Trammer, about the dark shadows in his eyes. Not only had he been through the hell of war, he had also suffered the tragic loss of a woman he loved. No wonder he had a maturity beyond other young men she met on the campus. She could better understand his driving obsession with film making, too. Tragedy such as he had known could ignite deep, storm-driven flames that become a powerful motivating force. Along with grief, he might be living with the torture of guilt over the death of the girl.

Now she found herself with a whole new set of emotions, a strange mixture of compassion for Kirk, sadness for the beautiful girl. But this unexpected development did little to clarify her thoughts about her own relationship with Kirk. If anything, she was only more uncertain and disturbed.

The crowd began thinning. By eleven o'clock, the last couple left. She was alone in the house with Kirk. He had collapsed on a lumpy old couch in the room that had the projection equipment. He was puffing on a cigarette, watching the smoke curl toward the ceiling.

She sat beside him, gazing at his rumpled hair, the

dark circles under his red-rimmed eyes, the lines of fatigue etching his features. An unexpected wave of caring engulfed her. "You look tired, Kirk. You need to get some rest."

A corner of his mouth smiled. He blew a smoke ring, watched it circle above him and dissipate. "I don't think I'll be able to sleep for a week. What did you think of the film, Natalie?"

"Why are you asking me? You ought to know by the reaction of all your friends. Everybody said it's breathtaking."

There was something boyish about his grin. "I want to hear you say it."

"All right. I'm certainly not a critic. I'm not as hep about this film-making business as your friends in the cinema department. I'm an actress. But I thought it was absolutely superb. I don't know when I've been so moved."

Despite his state of near-exhaustion, for the present moment the haunting shadows were gone from his eyes. In their place was an expression of burning triumph. "The color balance is still off in places, but the lab can fix that. Otherwise . . . yeah, I guess it isn't too bad."

Natalie couldn't control her hands. She had to touch him. Her fingers reached out, gently traced the lines of his face, trailing down from his temple to the stubble of beard on his jaw. They moved to the moist corner of his lips. A shiver coursed through her.

He crushed his cigarette in a tray beside the couch; then he captured her hand, pressed it against his cheek. His eyes held hers captive for a long moment as he slowly moved her hand to his lips. One by one he kissed her fingers. He turned her hand over. She felt the tickle of the tip of his tongue. Her breath caught in her throat with a stifled gasp. Her heart had begun a steady, pounding tempo, sending waves of warm blood through her body, making her flesh tingle.

She became acutely aware of how close she was to him. Sitting beside him, her hip pressed against his side. It was a burning contact.

He released her fingers. His hand dropped to her knee. Her eyes widened. She saw a questioning look in his gaze; she couldn't answer it. Her eyes closed. She sucked in her breath through parted lips as his touch strayed from her knee to her inner thigh. Sensations cascaded through her. Pulsating waves of heat began within the recesses of her being and spread through her.

His other arm went around her and gently drew her into his embrace. For a long moment, their eyes were inches apart. She felt his breath on her lips. She was breathing hard, her heart pounding. She had never felt this way with a man before. The nightmare of childhood had haunted her all these years, locking passion behind closed doors of her psyche. She had thought she would never become a whole woman and had accepted her fate, to play out love scenes on a stage that she would never feel in real life.

Even now there was a war being waged within her. Desire was so new to her it was frightening. A dam was threatening to break inside, drowning her in emotions and sensations that she had never before known.

Ever so slowly, he drew her closer and closer. After

what seemed an eternity, his lips just barely met hers, a feather touch. Again and again they touched that way, light as a moonbeam, gently making contact until her own mounting desire demanded more and her mouth locked hungrily with his.

His arms became steel bands around her. She welcomed the pressure. Her breasts were mashed against his muscular chest. He had pulled her all the way down until now she could feel the entire length of his body beneath her. The quivering flesh of her thighs felt the warmth of his burning through their clothing. She knew the intimate contact of her stomach, soft against the muscular ridges of his abdomen.

His caress moved down the small of her back, exploring the curves of her hips, testing the yield of soft flesh under mashing fingers. She felt herself growing faint with longing.

From her lips, his kisses traced a fiery trail along the soft curve of her cheek to the hollow of her throat. He gently nuzzled the curves of her bosom. Her breasts suddenly throbbed with an aching fullness. She found his caress unbearably sweet, bringing tears to her eyes. Churning emotions gripped her heart.

With a slow, gentle sweetness that annihilated her muffled objections, he opened her blouse. His searching fingers found their way under her bra, cupping the delicate, pale curves he found there.

"Natalie . . ." he whispered in a voice thick with desire.

He had awakened desire that now raged through her in a molten flood. Never . . . never had she dreamed in her wildest fantasies that she could experience such wanton hunger. Her flesh yearned for his flesh. Her breasts ached to rest naked against his strong, broad chest. Her thighs quivered to feel themselves pressed against his. She groaned with the hunger he had aroused.

Natalie wrenched her mouth from his, panting. She was on the brink of something so vast and overwhelming that she was terrified, and began shivering uncontrollably.

His hands moved up, cupped her face. He gave her a long, serious look, then gently pushed her head against his shoulder, stroking her hair and cuddling her until the shivering subsided.

"I'm—I'm not very good at this," she apologized. "I've never been with a man before."

There was a surprised silence. She was aware of his questioning gaze and buried her flushed face against his shoulder. Her voice was muffled. "Don't ask me to explain. It has to do with something that happened to me as a child. I freeze up around men. It's different with you. I hadn't expected anything like this to happen. I wasn't prepared for it."

He slowly sat up, his face serious. "Neither was I, to be frank. I guess first impressions aren't very valid. When I first met you I saw a cool, poised, golden-haired beauty whose diction was right out of the finest East Coast finishing school, clothes from Saks Fifth Avenue, name in the social register . . . yacht races, limousines . . . trips to Europe. What does this type want with a guy like me? Slumming perhaps?"

"You snob!" she chided gently.

"Maybe." He grinned wryly. "But it's a valid question. Why me?"

"I don't know. Why me? You're a fascinating, sexy

man. You could have your pick of co-eds on the campus."

He shrugged. "I don't have time for that kind of stuff."

I'm glad to hear that, she thought.

There was a moment of silence. "Cigarette?" he offered.

"Thanks. I don't smoke."

He picked up a crumpled pack from the floor beside the couch, but put it back down without taking a cigarette. "Maybe," he said, "it's the insanity of the evening. We're all a little high over seeing the finished job on the film."

"Yes, maybe." His words made her feel letdown.

He gazed at her intently. "Well, Natalie Brooks, we are facing a decision. Are we going to see each other some more?"

"I—I guess that's up to you."

"Is it?"

She avoided his eyes, her cheeks warm, unable to deal with the question.

"Well," he said slowly, taking her hand, "if it's up to me, I say, yes, I want to see you some more. But you'd better not rush into this without thinking it over. You're not the type to become involved in a casual affair. Do you really want to get your life all tangled up with a guy like me? What would your family and your friends in the social register say?"

Natalie raised her eyes. Face flushed, she said softly, "It's my life. It's not my family's decision."

From that moment on, it was like hooking a ride on a fast express. At times she wondered if she had ever truly been alive before she met Kirk. He lived his life as if it were scenes from a movie script. When working on a movie, he could shoot scenes all day and stay up editing all night until he finally collapsed and slept around the clock. He played as hard as he worked. They dashed around the country to student film festivals where Kirk's movies won award after award. He took her with him to a hot-air balloon meet which he was hired to film as a documentary. Somehow he got the use of one of the balloons and took Natalie on her first balloon ride. They drank champagne and kissed in the basket, high above the patchwork of fields. They went on wild dune buggy rides across the desert, stopped in the wilderness to have a picnic and make love in the shade of a Joshua tree.

Somewhere in the whirlwind of events, they got married. As Kirk warned, Natalie's family and friends on the East Coast were dismayed. Who was Kirk Trammer? Natalie was too much in love to be concerned.

But sometimes she asked herself the same question. Who, really, was Kirk Trammer? She was constantly finding out new things about him. She hadn't known he was an accomplished amateur magician until he pulled some of his sleight of hand prestidigitations on her without warning. It was just one of those things he'd dabbled in since a kid, he'd explained with a shrug. When working on a movie idea, he would spend hours at the piano, playing furiously, getting a feeling for mood from his music. There were times he would lapse into a brooding silence, withdrawn from her and the world. Those times she felt shut out from his life. The longer she was with him, the more she wondered if she would ever really know Kirk. He was a complex individual, tormented by drives and creative impulses that baffled her. With all her polish and finishing school sophistication, Natalie was by contrast a simple, direct girl.

After graduation, Kirk got his first break with a major studio. Impressed by his student films and documentaries, the studio agreed to finance a low-budget motion picture he would produce and direct. It was a simple story about a young soldier coming home from Viet Nam, trying to find his way back into the small-town life he had left. He shot the film on location with an unknown cast in less than four weeks. The motion picture was titled *The Home Front*. To everyone's surprise, most of all the studio executives', it became a cult movie among young audiences and ended up earning the studio a huge profit and turning Kirk into a rich young man overnight.

Meanwhile, Natalie's acting career was blooming. She had caught the eye of an advertising executive at one of the school's drama workshops. His company was actively producing commercials for national TV networks. She was offered a part in a cosmetic commercial. It was successful and was followed by a part in an hour special TV drama. That was when she acquired Ira Bevans as her agent. From then on her acting career took off like a skyrocket. A major role in a TV series led to a part in a motion picture and, almost overnight, Natalie Brooks became a promising young star.

That was when Kirk invented a nickname for her that she hated—"Lucky." He told her, "Remember when I told you you are one of the lucky ones? Life smiles on people like you. Sunshine is going to follow you wherever you go, Lucky. All you have to do is touch something and it turns to gold.''

For a while they lived a love story out of a movie scenario, two beautiful young people with the world at their feet. They went to the south of France for a second honeymoon, then bought the huge old mansion in Beverly Hills and spent a fortune remodeling it.

But their love story had an unhappy ending. Kirk embarked on a major motion picture production that was to become a disaster. Carrying the title *The Two of Us*, it was both the sweeping drama of a young woman's tumultuous career as a rock singer set against the background of the 1960s protest era, and her love story. Originally budgeted at $12 million by Continental Films, halfway through the film, because of Kirk's ambitious demands, it became obvious that the cost was going to be double that. Continental threatened to scrap the production unless Kirk would personally guarantee the loans they took out to complete the production. Kirk agreed to sink all of his capital into the film, certain it would be another money-maker like *The Home Front*. Some critics liked it. Audiences did not. It was a financial disaster. The studio lost a lot of money. Kirk lost all his money.

The film cost Natalie more than money. When she read the screenplay, it was obvious to her that *The Two of Us* was Kirk's own tragic love story with Jacqueline Davis. Natalie felt betrayed by the film. She tried to talk Kirk into dropping the project, but he plunged into it with a burning intensity that broke her heart. He became totally immersed in the production, shutting her out of his life.

At that time Natalie's acting career was taking her out of town much of the time. She didn't want to be separated from Kirk, but she had no choice. After *The Two of Us* cost Kirk his entire bankroll, they were living off her acting income. Kirk became even more of a stranger to her. With the colossal flop of *The Two of Us,* Kirk's career hit the skids. He roamed around the Beverly Hills mansion, his eyes looking burned out and empty. When he tried to call studio executives about doing another film he could not longer get past secretaries. "He's in a conference. I'll have him get back to you." They never called back. He didn't even have any luck finding a lesser job in a production department. He had been quickly typed as a flash in the pan, a young film school whiz kid who'd made a lucky strike with his first production, but he was temperamental, stubborn, unpredictable. The studio blamed him for unrealistically sinking a huge budget into a film that had no mass appeal.

Gossip tabloids hinted that Kirk now had a drinking problem, was spending his wife's money in bars and was having an affair with the actress who had starred in his ill-fated movie. Natalie never found out if there was any truth to the rumors. She flew home from the East Coast one weekend to find a note from Kirk saying that he had left for Europe. "So long, Lucky. You'll be okay. Remember what I told you. You're one of the ones life smiles on. Wherever you go, sunshine will follow you. Whatever you touch will turn to gold."

There had been no hint of ever wanting to see her again. He'd made no move to contact her during the two years he had been away.

Suddenly he had returned from Europe and walked back into her life again, dropping a fresh emotional bombshell into her existence.

Chapter Four

*N*ow at the Dentmens' Malibu beach house party, Natalie looked around at her friends, shaking her head in bewilderment. "Kirk wants me to star in his new film? You can't be serious."

"We're very serious," Bill Dentmen insisted. "We all want you to take the part, Natalie. We've always wanted to work together as a team. This is our opportunity."

Natalie fought back tears. "It's out of the question."

"Won't you at least read his story synopsis?" Linda persisted. "The part is perfect for you."

"I don't care if it's the greatest part in the world," Natalie said heatedly. "The last thing I want to do is put myself in a position of having Kirk direct a film in which I would act. The next time I get anywhere near Kirk Trammer it will be in a divorce court!"

There was a moment of silence. Then Bill said gently, "Look, Natalie, we're more than friends, we're like family. So maybe I can say this—we don't know what went wrong with you and Kirk. It started out so great, just like the perfect romantic screenplay, two lovers made for each other. I guess, like in so many Hollywood marriages, the odds were stacked against you. Each of you had your own careers. Kirk's future seemed to hit the skids about the time you started making it big. Maybe Kirk's pride couldn't take that. Maybe he just had to get away to find a new direction, get his feet back on the ground. Going to Europe was good therapy for him. The critics over there hold him in much higher esteem than those here in the States. His film that bombed out at the box offices here won awards at European film festivals. Kirk got his morale back. He directed several documentaries over there that were extremely well done. He's changed, Natalie. He's got his confidence back. This story he brought back with him could put him on top of the business where he belongs. You know I've always thought Kirk was a genius."

"Bill, I know you're probably Kirk's best friend and a great admirer of his," Natalie said sullenly. "Maybe he is a genius, another Orson Welles, or something. I just don't want to have anything more to do with him. He's caused me enough grief. Anyway, this conversation is pointless. My agent told me all about this film Kirk wants to produce and direct. He said there isn't a studio in Hollywood that will touch the project with a ten-foot pole."

Bill nodded soberly. "It's true that so far he hasn't been able to get anyone to finance the project. But it would make a big difference if you agreed to play the lead. You've become such big box office that a studio would think twice before turning down a chance to produce the next Natalie Brooks film, even if Kirk Trammer is the director."

Natalie's eyes widened. Suddenly she was furious. "So that's why he's persuaded you to try and talk me into doing the part in his film! He wants to use me to get a studio to take on his project. That lousy rat! It's just the sort of thing Kirk Trammer would pull!"

"Don't be too hard on Kirk, Natalie," her cousin, Ginny, interjected. "We're all kind of guilty, I guess. Remember, back in school we made a pact to help each other. Whoever made it big in the industry would help the others so we could put our own production company together. Well, we've all done okay. We've all had our screen credits. But you're the one who really hit the big time in a hurry. I know it's selfish of us to try to twist your arm over this, but it would be a great opportunity for all of us."

Natalie glared at her cousin. "You're not fair, putting me on the spot like that! If it were anybody except Kirk, you know I'd do anything to help you guys. I owe you. You were the first really close friends I ever had. And I'd love to have our own production company. It would be fantastic to do some of the things we've talked about, to have the creative freedom without a bunch of studio executives getting in the way. But I'd just be letting myself in for a fresh load of grief with Kirk."

"Couldn't you just deal with him on a professional level? Keep your personal lives out of it?" Ginny asked.

"Ha!" Natalie sneered. "You know what dealing with Kirk Trammer on a film set is like. Swimming around in a tank full of sharks is easier on the nerves. There is no such thing as staying impersonal with that man."

"Well, look, Natalie," Bill said, "do this much for us. Take the story home. Look it over. Kirk is on the East Coast this week, checking on some possible financing. He'll be back on Friday. We're going to get together here again Friday night and kick this whole thing around some more. Give it some prayerful consideration in the meantime and come out on Friday. Maybe by then you'll reconsider."

He had sentenced her to a number of sleepless nights. When she got home, she read Kirk's story synopsis.

The title was *The Last Encounter*. It was a love story played out against a background of international intrigue. The hero was Clay Winters, a dashing space-age scientist. The heroine was Rebecca Abrahms, an Israeli news correspondent. The other woman in the story was a beautiful, dark-eyed Russian KGB agent, Nichole Nikova.

There were dramatic visual effects as the story opened with scenes in outer space. In the story the American space program is completing work on a giant space station. There would be shots of the space shuttles, astronauts working in space suits and dramatic views of the interior of the space station. Clay Winters is a civilian scientist employed by NASA. He meets Rebecca Abrahms on the space station. She is with a news media group that has arrived by space shuttle to write firsthand news stories about the space station.

The station will play a decisive role in world peace: it contains a sensing device which can discover a nuclear rocket launch anywhere in the world and immediately destroy it with a laser beam. Thus it has ended the threat of nuclear war, and all the world powers have dismantled their nuclear warheads.

Clay Winters, who played an important part in the design and construction of the space station, meets Rebecca Abrahms and falls in love with her. There is something mysterious about the woman. Rebecca's parents were killed in a bombing raid. Her husband was captured by the Syrians and she doesn't know if he's dead or alive. She tries not to become involved with Clay Winters. After completing her news story on the space station, she flies to Rio de Janeiro on another assignment. Clay follows her there. There are love scenes between Clay and Rebecca shot during the colorful four-day Mardi Gras-type Carnival.

At this point the beautiful Russian KGB agent, Nichole Nikova, enters the story. She encounters Clay and warns him that there is a plot to destroy the space station. A small Middle-Eastern country such as Iran has developed a nuclear weapon. If that country can eliminate the space station guardian device, it can then blackmail the major powers with the threat of sending the nuclear rocket to destroy major cities. Nichole believes Rebecca has knowledge of the plot. Rebecca again flees, this time to the Middle East, where the story builds to a climax in a setting of that strife-torn region.

It was as Bill described, a potential blockbuster.

From a professional standpoint, Natalie thought she would have no qualms about accepting the lead role. It could be the biggest movie of the year. But that did not alleviate her conflict. How could she agree to an arrangement that would put her in daily contact with Kirk? Every day would turn into a devastating, heart-wrenching experience.

She tossed and turned. Sleep was out of the question. From a standpoint of self-interest, the solution was obvious: She should firmly refuse to have anything to do with the matter. But that's where the conflict came in. She thought about her friends who saw this as the opportunity they had dreamed about, a chance to form their own movie company. And there was Kirk. What would become of him if every studio turned him down? Would he ever get another opportunity to direct a major film? Would it be the final blow to his career?

Then she asked herself, why should it matter to her? Why should she get involved? She owed Kirk nothing. Why cause herself more grief over him?

Did she have some feeling left for him, enough so that she couldn't just stand by and see his dreams die? After all, she had shared her life with him for six years. No matter how angry she was with him, she couldn't completely wipe that out. Being married somehow left the indelible imprint of the other person on one's life forever.

She dreaded to see Friday come around. Her emotions were in a turmoil. She didn't want to go back to Malibu, but she couldn't stay away. Again she dressed in beach clothes, a different sarong-and-swimsuit combination. She spent extra time with her hair and makeup. Knowing that she was going to meet Kirk face-to-face was causing her the worst case of stage fright she had ever experienced. Her emotions were a battleground of anticipation and dread. A half dozen times on the way out to Malibu, she stopped her car to turn around. But a force stronger than her will took over and steered the car back on its fateful journey. Her hands on the wheel were like ice. Her knuckles were white.

She arrived at the Dentmens' house early and had a drink with Sally and Bill, chatting nervously as the others arrived, first Linda Towers, then Ginny Wells. There appeared to be an unspoken agreement to steer clear of the subject of Kirk and the movie project.

They were on the deck about sunset when she caught sight of a familiar figure striding up the beach toward them.

All of her senses froze. Her breath was suspended. Her first response was that her eyes were playing a trick on her. Many times in the past two years she had seen a tall, broad-shouldered man at a distance and thought for certain it was Kirk, only to have him turn around to reveal a total stranger. But this person drew closer and his features became clearer and there could no longer be a mistake.

Yes, it was Kirk.

He came up on the deck, flashing a smile, greeting everyone by name. His attire was like always, casual and rumpled as if he considered clothing no more than an irritating necessity. He had made a concession to the beach setting by wearing canvas deck shoes instead of his usual run-down Western boots. His tan sport shirt hung loose and unbuttoned. A piece of cord took the place of a belt at the waist of his sailcloth beach slacks. He looked like a suntanned beachcomber.

Natalie was overwhelmed by a jumble of impressions: his strong, tanned forearms, the impatient fingers brushing back the rebellious shock of dark hair, the blazing, golden hazel eyes that sent a jolt through her like a lightning bolt.

It was an awkward moment for both of them. But Kirk managed to break the ice. "Hello, Natalie," he said in an even voice.

Natalie swallowed hard and nodded, unable to use her voice. She had instinctively risen to her feet, perhaps from a primitive instinct to flee. Her legs trembled, barely able to support her. Time had dimmed somewhat her remembrance of how she could be overwhelmed by his presence. Now the memory came back in a rush. The familiar scent of his cologne, the magnetism that radiated from him like a force field, the almost imperceptible heat of his body, reminded her with nerve-shattering clarity of the impact he had on her. She tried to drag her gaze from his but couldn't. God, don't let him touch me, she prayed. But he did. His hand reached out hesitantly and made contact with hers, sending agonizing shock waves through her body.

Her flesh came alive with memories of his touch. Her breasts tingled, affected by the countless times his hands had cupped them and his lips had known their yielding curves and taut nipples.

She reacted to the exquisite shock of his touch with a wave of longing that made her dizzy. She was furious with herself that she would respond like this.

Hadn't he hurt her enough? But reason didn't matter. She did still want him in the same old way. Was she still in love with him? It was not a question she could answer. Perhaps he had killed that, but the primitive desire for him was as overwhelming and fresh as the first time they had made love. *Oh, damn him!* she thought helplessly. No other man could ever arouse her as he could.

Drinks and hors d'oeuvres were served. There was an obviously strained attempt at bright conversation. Natalie sat huddled in her chair, a glass clutched in her cold hands.

She found it impossible not to look at Kirk. As Bill had said, the sojourn in Europe had been good for him. He looked tanned and healthy. It was easy to see that his morale had been restored.

He was slouched comfortably in a deck chair, looking totally relaxed. His unbuttoned shirt hung open, revealing the bared ridges of chest muscles. Natalie's gaze was drawn hypnotically from his chest down to his navel and the whirl of hair just below and she was conscious of a fresh, thick clutch of desire. Furious with her own weakness, she gulped her drink, then had a temporary coughing spell as she became strangled.

At one point in the conversation, he turned to her. "I saw a preview of *Never Tomorrow*. In spite of the fact that they handled most of the scenes all wrong, your acting saved the picture. Congratulations."

"I suppose you would have directed the picture differently?" she said coolly.

"Certainly. I can't understand the studio spending

money on a production like that and hiring someone like Will Baxley to direct. He should be running a public relations office instead of directing a major film."

Natalie felt a sting of annoyance at Kirk's cocksure attitude. At the same time, she had to admit he was right. Baxley was a miserable director. Only expert editing had saved the picture. She mentally compared Baxley's style with Kirk's. Will Baxley's main concern was staying in the good graces of the studio heads, keeping within the budget and shooting-time schedule, and keeping the cast in a good mood. He often let them flounder through a scene with no real sense of purpose while he was leaning over backward not to. ruffle anyone's feelings. Kirk, on the other hand, was a dictator on the set. He kept everyone, from the stars to the gaffers, in a turmoil. He demanded the effect he was striving for, refusing to settle for one iota less than perfection.

"Tell us about Europe, Kirk," Sally Dentmen exclaimed in an effort to steer the conversation toward safer, less personal ground.

Natalie was grateful that she could avoid further dialogue with Kirk. She drew back in the shadows, allowing the party to center around Kirk and the others. She put her drink down and quietly slipped away, strolling down to the beach along the water's edge. A full moon cast its silver light over the sand and glistening waves. A soft breeze stirred her hair and played with her sarong as she walked. She was trying to grasp some composure from the peaceful scene around her.

Suddenly a hand touched her arm. She gasped and spun around. Kirk's figure, a tall silhouette in the moonlight, confronted her.

"Sorry, Lucky. Didn't mean to frighten you," he murmured.

Despite the shadows, she could feel his burning gaze rake her, from her wind-tossed hair down to her bare midriff. Instinctively, she reached down to clasp the sarong that had parted above the knees to reveal the curves of her legs.

"I wish you wouldn't call me that nickname," she said irritably. "You know I don't like it."

"I forgot. Fits you, though. Things are going real fine for you careerwise, the way I predicted. Everything you touch turns to gold."

"Why did you follow me?" she demanded.

"You wanted to be alone?"

"Wasn't it obvious that's why I left the party?"

There was a strained silence as their gazes clashed. He sighed. "Natalie, I can understand how you feel, but we need to talk. Bill said they've discussed with you the matter of your playing the lead in the film we're going to do."

"Yes."

"What have you decided?"

"I haven't made a decision. I don't really think I should do it."

"Why not? It's a fine part for you. Have you read the story synopsis?"

"Yes. It's a good story. I can see the possibilities. But I don't like the idea of being used. You only want me for the part because you know that's the only way you're going to get a studio to take on your project."

He scowled darkly. "That's not true. All of us agree the part is made for you. I don't need your help to get studio backing."

"You're whistling in the dark. My agent told me there isn't a studio on the West Coast that will touch you with a ten-foot pole."

"Ira would say that. He never had any use for me. Still, if you like the story and the part, what difference does it make? The production could do a lot for your career as well as ours. It would benefit us all." He grinned crookedly. "Maybe some of your luck would rub off."

Natalie fought hard to hold back her tears. "I think at this point what would benefit me most would be to end this farce of a marriage. It's really our lawyers who need to talk, don't you agree?"

His face grew darker than the shadows. He frowned, impaling her with a fierce look. "I don't remember saying anything about a divorce."

Natalie shook her head in disbelief. "You take off for Europe for two years. I don't hear one word from you. Do you have the gall to think you can casually come back when the mood strikes you and find me waiting with open arms?"

He looked out across the moving waves, a dark grimace crossing his face. "It was a turning point in my life, my career. Everything went sour for me. I had run into a stone wall. I was desperate. I wasn't any good to you or myself anymore. I had to be by myself for a while, to sort matters out, to get my life back on track. If you love me, you should understand that."

"If somebody loves somebody, he doesn't desert

them," she choked, no longer able to control her tears.

"Natalie, take your share of the blame. You know our marriage was coming apart at the seams. You were all wrapped up in your career. You were gone all the time."

All the bitter memories of their separation brought an angry retort to her lips. She thought about his motion picture, *The Two of Us,* a tribute to his lost love, Jacqueline, and how it had hurt and humiliated her. And she remembered the ugly gossip about Kirk and the actress who had played the lead in his film. But she swallowed the words. She was not going to lower herself to a name-calling harangue.

Kirk's gaze suddenly swung back to her, immobilizing her with fierce intensity. There were times he could look at her so ferociously, it frightened her. He said hoarsely, "It's no easier for me to live with you than for you to live with me—you with that cool, iceberg reserve they taught you in finishing school. We're two volatile, creative people, Natalie. Putting us in the confines of marriage is like trying to contain a forest fire."

There was a moment of silence as tense as high wires strained to the breaking point. Suddenly he grasped her arms, pulled her close. Wide-eyed she stared up at his face, inches away, seeing his angrily knotting jaw, the fire raging in his eyes. Then his mouth came down on hers with a fierce, savage hunger. She was totally his captive. If she were an iceberg, the fire of his kiss was a torch cutting through the ice. She was like a helpless doll in his powerful arms. She felt every curve of her body pressed against his relentless masculine physique. Rational thought was blotted out. She dissolved into a universe of emotion and sensation. She heard her own gasp as his lips stirred the embers of repressed passions. His hands slid down her back, as if seeking to remember the curves. Her heart pounded. She tried to protest as she became aware of his fingers slipping under the waistband of her sarong in search of her quivering hips.

"Don't . . ." she gasped.

But he continued to explore relentlessly the curves, creases and hollows under her sarong, his palms moving over quivering bare flesh, seeking out remembered secrets. Her breath was rasping in her throat as he pulled her halter top down. The damp, salty air washed over her bared breasts. He nuzzled her bosom, then tasted the pink-tipped fruits of their lush globes.

Natalie dug her fingers in his hair, gasping for breath, her body lurching against his. Her muscles had become liquid, drained of strength.

His chuckle was low and triumphant in his throat. "You still love me, Natalie."

"I don't," she choked, beginning to cry. "You destroyed that, Kirk." But she wondered if it was true.

"Whether you love me or not, you still want me like before, as much as ever!"

She had no answer for that. If she denied it, she would be lying. Right now, she desperately wanted him to take her—right here in the sand with the surf licking at their naked bodies and the stars overhead the canopy above their marriage bed of sand.

Instead, almost roughly, he thrust her away from him. She was shaken, her knees barely able to support her. Her heart was pounding harder than the surf around her feet. Kirk glared at her. "Remember that when you're talking to your lawyer about a divorce!" And he turned and stalked off into the darkness.

She crumpled to the beach, sobbing with humiliation and despair.

Natalie was glad that she had to fly to New York the following week for talk show interviews. It gave her a brief respite from the emotional turmoil Kirk's return had caused. She took the sunset flight out of Los Angeles. Speeding across the continent, she wrestled with the problem of what to do about her situation. By the time her trip was over she had decided on a compromise. She was not going to accept a part in the film, but she would use her influence with the studio to get backing for Kirk's film. She owed that much to her friends and for the past she had shared with Kirk.

Back in Los Angeles, she phoned the Dentmens. "Bill, I've given a lot of thought to this situation all the way to the East Coast and back and I've made a decision. I simply cannot accept a part in Kirk's picture. But I will see if I can talk the studio into taking on the project. There's a young vice-president at Continental Films who might go for it. His name is Jim Hanley. He brought the *Never Tomorrow* property to the studio and all indications are that it's going to make Continental a pile of money. So right now Jim carries a lot of weight down there. If I can sell him on the project he might be able to get Sam Kasserman, the studio head, to take it on. At least it's worth a try.

Bill's voice registered his disappointment. "We've all been hoping you'd accept the role, Natalie. It's perfect for you. We want you on the team. Is there anything I can say that would make you reconsider?"

"Sorry. My mind is made up. You can find someone else to do the part. The important thing is to get studio backing, right?"

"Well, of course that's essential if we're going to go into production," Bill admitted. "Despite the changes that have come to Hollywood it's still the major studios who control the industry. Even if Kirk could get financing from some other source, he still needs the distribution only a major studio can provide. No need to tell you that. But we were hoping we could all be in this together."

"I just can't deal with it, Bill. But I will call Jim Hanley first thing in the morning. Now we're going to need more than a synopsis. Can you and Sally work up a story treatment for me to show him?"

"Sure, we'll get to work on it right away."

Chapter Five

$\mathcal{N}$atalie, there's going to be an executive story conference this afternoon. I think you'd better come down."

Natalie had taken the story treatment of Kirk's property to Jim Hanley a week ago. She'd had no response from him until her phone rang this morning.

"What did you think of the story?" Natalie asked.

"Well, it may have potential," the vice-president hedged.

"Did you show it to Sam Kasserman?"

"Yes. It's been on his desk for several days."

"Has he said how he feels about it?"

Hanley's response was guarded. "He hasn't said, Natalie. But he's bringing it up in the conference this afternoon. That's why I thought you might want to be there. Sam loves you. We all do. Sam will want to talk to you personally about it. He wants to hold the meeting at three this afternoon. Okay?"

That was all she could get out of the studio executive at that point.

Shortly before three that afternoon, Natalie pulled into the lot of Continental Films. She found a parking place near the administration buildings. She glanced around at the buildings housing the sound stages, the equipment storage units, the outdoor sets, the commissary, all the elements of a studio lot that made up its own community. Then she walked to the main building where the office of the studio president was located.

All of the executive power of the studio was gathered in Sam Kasserman's office that afternoon, vice-presidents, various department heads, secretaries. When Natalie entered the large, mahogany-paneled room, the men jumped to their feet. She was welcomed with the eager homage and affection due a queen. Kasserman hurried around from behind his desk to embrace her and kiss her cheek. "Natalie, my darling. How sweet of you to come down." He led her to a comfortable, plush chair beside his desk and seated her with a flourish. Then he resumed his place behind his desk. Natalie thought with amusement that the meeting had the overtones of a royal court. Kasserman, the studio head, was on his throne behind his massive desk. Around the room in various levels of importance were the knights, the lords and the vassals of his kingdom.

From across the room, Jim Hanley smiled and nodded a greeting. At thirty, Hanley had already reached the level of senior vice-president in charge of physical production. On his shoulders rested the enormous, complex nuts and bolts of motion picture production. It was Hanley's office that procured the automobiles, furniture, horses, guns, lumber, airplanes—all the hardware that was the raw material of movie sets. Then he managed somehow to get all the material to the right location when it was needed. Details of transportation for camera crews, production staffs and actors were Hanley's responsibility. An even greater responsibility, one upon which his job depended, was monitoring films in production and keeping a zealous lid on expenses.

Natalie had decided to show Kirk's story treatment to Hanley first for diplomatic reasons. She could have taken the script directly to Sam Kasserman. But by showing it first to Jim Hanley she had flattered him and had given him the opportunity to make a professional score if the film turned out to be a hit. Thus, she already had one executive at least tentatively on her side. She was very much aware of the powerful egos involved in the studio hierarchy and the constant, ongoing struggle for acclaim and recognition. Getting credit for a movie success was as important for a studio executive as an Academy nomination to an actress. It had been a feather in Hanley's cap that he brought the *Never Tomorrow* property to the attention of the studio. It was only natural that he would be eager to add another successful property to his list. It was that kind of thing that caught the attention of the real power behind the throne—the corporate owners of the studio in New York.

Sam Kasserman interrupted her thoughts. "Well,

Natalie, darling, before we say anything else, I have to tell you that it looks like we got a winner in *Never Tomorrow*. The first week's rental figures have come in from all over the country and let me say that they look most encouraging."

White-haired and deeply tanned, Kasserman was a distinguished man in his early sixties. He was always impeccably dressed. Today his eyes were sparkling and he rubbed his hands together as he talked. Obviously he was in a jubilant mood over the success of Continental's latest movie. That was a strike in favor of Kirk's story, she thought; she had caught Kasserman in a good mood.

As head of a large motion picture studio, Sam Kasserman held one of the most difficult jobs in Hollywood. His responsibilities were staggering. He had to try and guess a year and more in advance the fickle taste trends of film audiences; to choose from hundreds of possibilities the few productions that could be turned into successful motion pictures; to select the right director and producer; to evaluate how a picture was progressing in mid-production and if it wasn't progressing well, or running way over budget, what to do about it. It was his job to deal with the bankers who financed the films. He had to deal with temperamental people in a community of swollen and delicate egos. He made a steady stream of decisions about advertising campaigns, about timing releases for distribution not only in the United States but all over the world.

"That's real good news," Natalie said with a smile, replying to his enthusiastic news about her latest film.

"You did it again, sweetheart," Sam continued,

beaming. "They're standing in line to see Natalie Brooks. You made the picture."

"You're sweet to say that, Sam," Natalie replied. "But don't you think the writers, camera crew, producers, makeup people and all the rest had something to do with it?"

Kasserman dismissed her show of modesty with a generous wave of his hand. "Sure, we had good people on the film. But you were the star, Natalie."

She was not so naïve as to let the studio president's flattery go to her head. It was part of his role as father image to feed the egos of the people who worked for him. Natalie was sensible enough to know that at the moment she was riding a crest of popularity. But let her appear in a couple of box office duds and her position as a studio queen would come to an end. Suddenly the offers for juicy parts would stop. It would become more difficult to get into Sam's office. "He's in conference this morning, Miss Brooks; I'll have him get back to you," would become an impersonal secretary's polite door slam.

"I guess we timed things pretty good when I suggested you come down about three o'clock," he said. "We've gotten all our other business out of the way so you wouldn't have to sit through a lot of dull, boring talk that doesn't concern you, Natalie."

His vast, highly polished mahogany desk top was totally bare except for a gold-plated pen-and-pencil set, a picture of his wife and children, an ashtray and a file folder. Now he carefully adjusted the pen-and-pencil set, moved the picture an inch to the left, squared the file folder before him and opened it. He took out the story treatment of Kirk's film project, looked at the cover, his lips pursed, and put it down. He cleared his throat and swung his executive chair slightly to the left to face Natalie. "Well, Kirk is back from Europe."

Natalie nodded, hoping the rush of blood to her cheeks did not show. Until the mention of Kirk's name, she had been totally cool and reserved.

"I hope I'm not intruding on your personal life if I say I hope things are working out all right for you, Natalie. What the heck, we're all family here. I feel just like your father. So I guess I can ask. Have you and Kirk patched things up?"

"Not exactly," Natalie said uncomfortably. She knew Sam was putting out feelers to get a handle on where her marriage stood and how she was affected by it. At the moment she was a great asset to Continental Films. She added, "We're still separated if that's what you mean."

"Too bad. I was hoping things would smooth out for you, Natalie. But maybe it's for the best." He shrugged. "That's something you and Kirk have to work out," he said as he picked up the manuscript again. "I guess it's a friendly separation, though. Jim passed along this project of Kirk's. He said you brought it to him."

"Kirk and I are still friends," Natalie replied, choosing her words carefully. "I read the story and thought it had a lot of potential and that Continental should see it."

"Yes. We do appreciate your bringing it down. Of course, we already knew about it. Word gets around.

We heard Kirk came back from Europe with a movie he wants to do. This is the first chance I had to read it through.''

There was a moment of silence. One of the secretaries rustled a paper. An executive scowled at her.

Natalie asked, "Well, what do you think of the story?"

Kasserman sat back in his chair, frowning thoughtfully. He pursed his lips, leaned forward, studiously turned the pen-and-pencil set slightly to the left and moved the family picture an inch closer. He picked up the story treatment, held it for a moment, then carefully placed it in the file folder. *"The Last Encounter.* What can I say? It's got possibilities." He nodded. "Yes, I think I can definitely see it as a possibility as the next Natalie Brooks feature. Of course, we'd have to hold close reins on Kirk's spending. He has a bad reputation for going way over budget—"

"Just a minute, Sam," Natalie interrupted. "There's a little misunderstanding. I don't plan to accept a part in the film. I was just doing Kirk a favor by asking Continental to consider his proposal."

Natalie could feel the startled silence. It was as if the entire room took a sudden, quick breath. Sam Kasserman frowned. "I don't understand. Natalie, this would be a good film for you. Look, I've got to be frank. I don't have a whole lot of use for Kirk. Nobody is denying the man has a lot of talent. But he's a problem. That last thing he did, *The Two of Us,* cost the company a bundle. They're still screaming about it in New York. But we might overlook the problems I expect we'll have with Kirk if we can get you in this picture."

Natalie studied the expression on Kasserman's face. He would make a good poker player. Nevertheless, she knew exactly what was going on in his mind. She thought about the complex financial structure behind this modern Hollywood motion picture studio. Its roots were not here in sunny California but in the New York boardroom of the parent corporation, Atlantic Enterprises. Natalie was better acquainted with behind-the-scenes power struggles than many other Hollywood people working in the industry because of her family ties back East. Her great-uncle, Jeffrey Brooks, among other things, was on the board of directors of Atlantic Enterprises. He was one of the financial geniuses who had built the Brooks family fortune through shrewd financial wheeling and dealing. One of Natalie's early childhood memories was of Uncle Jeffrey taking her down to watch the activity on the floor of the New York Stock Exchange.

Continental Films was only part of the holdings of the parent conglomerate. Among the other corporations Atlantic Enterprises owned was a recording company, a book publisher and hotels in Atlantic City. They had recently acquired a home computer manufacturing concern for $50 million.

The late 1960s had been a time of vast change in the movie industry in Hollywood as the old studios originally founded by individuals and partners were taken over by corporate conglomerates, insurance and real estate firms. The power wielded by the moguls since silent film days fell into the hands of corporate lawyers and board chairmen. Still, the making of motion pictures was an esoteric operation not entirely understood by investors and businessmen. They hired people like Sam Kasserman to head the studios, and the industry went on much as before, except that now stars were no longer under long-term contracts to individual studios. Major films were often produced by independent companies who nevertheless turned to the studios for their financing and distribution.

Through her Great-Uncle Jeffrey, Natalie knew there was an ongoing power struggle between Sam Kasserman here on the West Coast and the president of Atlantic Enterprises in New York, David Clawson. The two men hated each other. It was a battle of giant egos. For the past three years, Continental Films had climbed out of the red to become a profitable enterprise. Last year the studio had shown a $50 million profit. Both men tried to claim credit for the turnaround. If it weren't for Kasserman's strong allies on the board of directors of Atlantic Enterprises, he knew Clawson would waste no time getting him fired.

Natalie knew all those thoughts were going through the studio president's mind right now, carefully weighing his own position in a deal involving huge sums of money. She felt certain he liked Kirk's story, saw the tremendous possibilities. But Sam's position was too tenuous to take a gamble with a director whose last film had been such a disaster.

"Kirk's first film, *The Home Front*, made a lot of money for the studio," Natalie pointed out.

"True, honey, but it was a low-budget little movie that happened somehow to click with the young crowd. Nobody expected it to do very much business.

It surprised everyone, including Kirk. But this project"—he rustled the story treatment papers—"is something entirely different. This is no low-budget film. Knowing the grand scale Kirk likes to operate on, we're talking twenty million at least, maybe a lot more. He'll want to shoot the thing on locations scattered all over the globe. The cost of the special effects alone would be astronomical." He shook his head. "Unless we can count on a big box office name to go with it, like yours, I can't see any way we could take that kind of a gamble."

Natalie sighed. "I'm sorry, Sam. But for personal reasons, which I'm sure you understand, I don't want to act in a film Kirk is going to direct."

Kasserman made a grand gesture. "Okay, we'll get a different director. We'll buy the property from Kirk for a flat fee and get you any director you want."

Natalie gasped. "You think Kirk would go for a deal like that? What would you give him for the property, a measly $50 thousand? You know Kirk Trammer better than that. He'd laugh in your face."

Kasserman raised an eyebrow. "From what I hear, at the moment, fifty grand might look pretty good to Kirk. He's been broke for the past two years."

"There's only one way anybody is going to do Kirk's picture," Natalie said angrily. "He's going to produce and direct it and he's going to want a big percentage of ownership—"

She stopped in mid-sentence. *I'm doing it again!* she thought, aghast. *I'm taking Kirk's side, fighting for his interests.*

Badly shaken, she gathered up her purse and rose. "I appreciate the time you took to read the material,

Sam. If you want to make some kind of deal with Kirk, you can get in touch with him. As far as my acting in the film goes, I'm afraid it's out of the question."

"Well, that's too bad, Natalie, darling," Kasserman said, rising. "I'm sure you understand our position. If you change your mind, please contact us."

Natalie drove out of the gate of Continental Films feeling depressed and frustrated. She was impatient with herself for becoming this emotionally involved over the matter.

From the Continental studios, Natalie drove to Special Effects Unlimited, Inc., the independent business Ginny inherited when her father died. Natalie found her cousin on one of the sound stages where a miniature city complete to the tiniest detail was being constructed. "Hi. Do you have time for a coffee break?"

Ginny, wearing a blue jumpsuit and a scarf around her head, looked disheveled and harassed. "Just what I need," she exclaimed. "This thing is driving me nuts. You guys keep working on that park area until you get it right," she told the crew hovered over the miniature set. "Those trees look like something from a Barbie Doll kit!"

She paused before a mirror and muttered under her breath as she wiped a smudge from her freckled nose. Then she grabbed Natalie's arm and led the way to the coffee shop.

Seated in a booth with drinks before them, Ginger asked, "Well, how did it go?"

Natalie shook her head. "It didn't. Sam Kasserman turned it down."

Ginger's lively countenance fell. "Oh, heck. We had big hopes—what's wrong with Kasserman anyway? Can't he see the fantastic possibilities of the story?"

Natalie sighed. "He's afraid to take the chance. Kirk's reputation isn't helping any. Sam thinks Kirk would run way over budget. It's too big a gamble. I think part of it is that Sam knows David Clawson is after his scalp. A costly blunder could give Clawson the leverage he needs with the board of directors to get Sam fired." Natalie paused, then added, "The only way he'd consider the project would be for me to take the lead role. He thinks my name would sell enough tickets to take out some of the risk."

Ginger toyed with her glass. "It would, you know. I wish you'd change your mind. It would be such a great part for you."

"It's asking too much. I'm a nervous wreck already. Why should I get so upset because they turned Kirk down?"

"Maybe because you still care what becomes of him," Ginger suggested softly.

Natalie sighed, blinking back tears. "It's true. And that's exactly why I don't want to put myself in a position of working on a picture with him, where I'd be around him every day. I'd just be asking for more heartbreak. Ginger, I've never talked about this with anyone before, but you and I are as close as sisters. Everybody thinks the trouble between Kirk and me began when he went off to Europe. That was just the last straw. The trouble with us began a long time ago. It was a mistake for us ever to get married in the first place when Kirk was still in love with somebody else."

Ginger looked startled. "But—"

"No, I didn't have a flesh-and-blood rival, Ginger. I don't believe Kirk ever got over his first love, Jacqueline Davis."

"The girl who was killed in the motorcycle accident?"

"Yes. They were planning to get married, you know. Kirk tried to forget her, but he never did. I think he hoped marrying me would help him get over her. When that didn't work, he tried to bring her back to life on the screen."

"His movie, *The Two of Us?*" Ginger asked in surprise.

"Certainly. You remember the plot. The hero in love with a beautiful, sensitive girl who wanted to be a singer and at the end she dies. It was the real-life story of Jacqueline Davis. He even cast Marsha Sanders, an unknown actress, for the lead. She's a dead ringer for Jacqueline!"

"You could be building this up in your mind, Natalie. Writers and movie producers sometimes use material out of their lives for the stories they create."

"It's more than that. Remember how Barbra Streisand said she created the father she longed to have when she wrote and directed *Yentl?* Kirk was reliving his past with Jacqueline while he was doing the film. Afterward, he had an affair with Marsha because she played the role so convincingly. To him she became Jacqueline."

Ginger exclaimed impatiently, "Surely you don't believe that scandal sheet gossip about Kirk and Marsha Sanders! There wasn't a word of truth in it."

"Are you positive?"

"Well, I guess I couldn't swear to it on the witness stand," Ginger admitted uncomfortably. "I just don't think it's true."

"At this point, it doesn't matter," Natalie stated wistfully. "By now there's too big a rift between Kirk and me to ever be patched up."

There was a pause in their conversation. Then Ginger said hopefully, "Continental Films isn't the only studio in town. Maybe Kirk can get backing somewhere else."

"Maybe, but I'm afraid it's going to be the same wherever he goes. Did somebody tell him I was showing the story treatment to Continental?"

"Yes, Bill told him he and Sally were doing the story treatment and you would try to interest Continental Films."

"Then he's pacing the floor, waiting to hear how it turned out." Natalie chewed her bottom lip. In spite of their breakup, she still cared enough about Kirk to want to be kind. "I'd better break the news to him as gently as I can. Do you know where I can reach him?"

"He's staying at a house about a mile down the beach from the Dentmens. Do you remember Toby Calkins, the cinematographer we went to school with?"

"Two-ton Toby?" Natalie smiled. "Sure, I remember him. Is he still fat?"

"Fatter. Anyway, he's done quite well since school. Right now he's chief photographer on a location job out of state. He lent his Malibu beach house to Kirk while he's away. I have the address. There's no phone, though."

They talked for a while longer, then Ginger had to

get back to work. Natalie gathered her courage and drove out to Malibu. Following Ginger's directions, she found the beach house where Kirk was staying.

She knocked on the door but there was no answer. She turned to leave, then saw Kirk coming across the beach. He had been swimming. She felt the quickening rhythm of her heart as her gaze was drawn to his lean, broad-shouldered figure clad only in swimming trunks. His days on the beach had given him a golden tan. His wet body glistened in the sunlight. Natalie saw the ripple of his muscles as he came toward her in long strides. He was breathing hard from the swim.

Her wide-eyed gaze was pulled magnetically to the lithe outlines of his body. Her pulse quickened at the sight of him almost naked. He looked like a golden Greek god. *A god of pagan desire,* she thought as her breath caught in her throat. It was impossible to pull her gaze from the sight of his moving legs, his muscled torso, his swinging hips, his broad, strong shoulders. How many times she had nestled her cheek against those shoulders! How often those strong arms had encircled her! How many times that magnificent body had pressed down on hers, asking for surrender gladly given!

Remembering all that now, she was clutched by the familiar surge of desire. She was enslaved by it.

"Well, this is an unexpected but pleasant surprise," he said, coming up to her. "Hello, Natalie."

Surely he must hear the hammering of her heart!

"Hello." She hoped the quiver in her voice had not been noticed.

A towel was draped around his neck. He rubbed his wet, unruly hair. "Come on in and have a drink."

She followed, marveling at her lack of willpower. Around him, she fell under a spell that robbed her of the ability to marshal her thoughts.

"Beer okay? That's all I seem to have on hand at the moment."

"That's fine."

He disappeared into the kitchen and returned shortly carrying two tall, frosted glasses filled with golden, foaming liquid.

Natalie sat tensely in a wicker chair near a great picture window that afforded a magnificent view of the ocean. But she was oblivious to the scenic vista. Kirk, still wearing only his swimming trunks, had taken his place on a couch that faced her. His long legs were sprawled in a comfortable position. He looked loose and relaxed. Natalie's traitorous thoughts remembered the strength in his arms and legs. She fought against remembering the intimate knowledge she had of him and failed. Flashbacks exploded in her mind like displays of fireworks: a montage of recollections; the texture of his skin; the faint stubble on his jaw rubbing her cheek; the pressure of his arms around her bare back; the straining of her body against his.

Her face grew hot. With a feeling of desperation, she asked herself what insane impulse had brought her out here alone. But then she never did have good sense where Kirk Trammer was concerned.

Now he was gazing at her with a bright, eager expression in his dark eyes. "Bill told me you were taking the story treatment to Continental this week. Have you heard from Sam Kasserman?"

Natalie's mouth felt dry. She took a sip of the drink

to moisten her lips. "Yes." She hesitated, then added, "That's why I came out to talk to you."

Kirk put his drink down and leaned forward expectantly. The look on his face wrenched Natalie's heart. There were moments when he could look almost boyish in his eagerness. This was one of those times. The full reality of this situation brought a sinking sensation to her stomach. It was frightening to consider how much Kirk had at stake here. His future hung in the balance. What would become of him now? Would he go back to Europe? Would he become defeated and fade into obscurity? No matter what people in the industry thought of Kirk—that he was temperamental, hard to deal with, impractical, extravagant—and no matter what grief her personal life with him had brought her, she knew that Kirk had a tremendous talent. Given the chance with this production, he could bring a whole new, original vision to the film industry. Now it was her bitter task to break the sad news.

She drew a breath, gathered her courage and said, "Kirk, I'm sorry. Kasserman turned it down."

A series of emotions flashed across Kirk's eyes—shock, pain, anger. He uncoiled his lanky, six-foot frame from the couch and paced the room, rubbing the back of his neck. He struck his left palm with his right fist. "That nearsighted jerk!" he exclaimed. "Can't he see the possibilities in this production?"

"It isn't that. He thinks it's a good story, Kirk. It's you he's afraid of."

"Yeah, I know," Kirk said impatiently. *"The Two of Us.* Is that going to haunt me the rest of my life?

Okay, it wasn't big box office. It was still a work of art. It won awards at film festivals all over Europe."

Natalie made a helpless gesture. It wasn't only the money the studio had lost on Kirk's second film; it was his reckless disregard of budget limitations and his stubborn independence that put him on the blacklist with studio heads.

"Well, to hell with Continental!" Kirk raged. "There are a dozen major studios in this city."

Natalie nodded. "Sure," she said, but her voice was hollow.

The anger suddenly dissolved from Kirk's eyes. He collapsed onto the couch, withdrawing into one of his dark, brooding silences.

Defeat was like a dark cloud settling over him. Natalie felt helpless and depressed. Finally she said, "Well, I have to be leaving."

With a visible effort, Kirk shook off his black mood. "Don't go yet, Natalie. Would you stick around and let me take you out for dinner? We could drive down the coast to that little seafood place you used to like so much."

Warning signals went off in Natalie's thoughts. But the look on Kirk's face melted her caution. His morale had suffered a dreadful blow. He desperately needed someone to be with him tonight.

"All right," she agreed against her better judgment.

"Give me a few minutes to take a shower and get dressed. There are some books and records over there, or the TV—"

"I'll be okay."

In a half hour he emerged from the bedroom, freshly showered and shaved, dressed in new, crisp slacks and sport shirt. He looked achingly handsome and masculine. The sight of him, so clean and bright and manly, smelling of a woody after-shave lotion, made her weak. Spending the evening with him was going to play havoc with her emotions. She was being an utter fool to do this.

But it was too late to back out now. She handed him the keys to her car. Sitting beside him as they sped down the freeway, she settled into her bucket seat, her gaze straying to his strong, capable fingers gripping the wheel. He took command of the vehicle the way he dominated a movie set. It gave her a sense of security, a feeling that he could protect her from any dangers of the outside world. It would be easy to relax her guard, to be lulled into forgetting the real danger was in surrendering to this false island of safety close to him.

The small seafood restaurant on the waterfront served excellent food and gave her a measure of privacy. They were seated in a secluded booth where their meal wouldn't be interrupted by movie fans.

"This reminds me of that place in the south of France," Kirk said. "We were riding high then, remember? *The Home Front* was breaking box office records. I had more money than I thought there was in the world. You had signed a contract to do the TV series. We chartered the yacht and anchored in the yacht basin in a little seacoast port. We went ashore to the same café every night. A family operated it. They cooked all our favorite dishes, got out their best wine."

"Yes, and the father would come over to the table and tell us hair-raising stories about his adventures in the French Underground during World War II. I think they were slightly exaggerated."

"It doesn't matter. They were still great stories. I think we got along with them so well because your finishing school French was so fluent. We'd get a little tipsy on all that good wine and afterward walk along the waterfront holding hands and then hurry to the cabin in our yacht and make love. Sometimes we'd lay out on the deck afterward in the moonlight, remember?"

Natalie's cheeks stung with sudden warmth. She heard the rhythm of her heartbeat in her ears quicken with the tender, sweet emotions his reminiscence had awakened. She averted her eyes, concentrating on her meal. She was suddenly furious with him for stirring up bittersweet memories and furious with herself for falling into the trap—a trap that had again ensnared her emotions, awakening a yearning that warmed her body and made her breasts ache.

She strained to keep the conversation impersonal for the rest of the meal. When they drove back to the beach house where he was staying, she sat as far away from him as possible. Yet it was impossible to escape the awareness of his physical being in the confines of the small car. The heat of his body seemed to fill the close quarters, enveloping her.

When they arrived at the beach, he parked the car on a bluff overlooking the house. There was a panoramic view from there of the expanse of beach and the ocean stretching to the horizon, all bathed in the moonlight's silvery patina. The view took her breath away. *Oh, no,* she thought, *everything's conspiring against me tonight.*

"That's the same moon that shone down on us in the south of France," Kirk said softly. He turned toward her. With a feeling of panic, she saw the dark oval of his face.

"Kirk, no," she said unsteadily.

She quickly opened her door and fled from the car. She stumbled down the bluff, her heels sinking in the soft sand, not stopping until she had reached the water's edge. Standing there, she welcomed the sea breeze that fanned her hair and cooled her heated face.

But then Kirk came up behind her, touching off a fresh wave of panic. He was carrying a half-full bottle of wine that he had brought with them from the restaurant. "How about coming up to the cabin for a nightcap?" he offered, holding up the bottle.

"No thank you."

"Not even one for the road?"

"No," she said unsteadily.

She took off her shoes and began walking along the rim of the surf, blindly aware that it was important to keep moving.

Kirk stayed doggedly at her side. He caught her arm, forcing her to stop and face him. "Well," he said, "since you won't come up to the cabin, for a drink, how about a toast right here? No sense in letting a bottle of perfectly good wine go to waste."

He raised the bottle in a kind of salute as his eyes gazed relentlessly into hers, turning her knees to water. "To all the memories we made together."

He had a sip from the bottle, then took a clean

handkerchief from his pocket, carefully wiped the rim and handed it to her.

"I'll drink to memories," she said, weakening. "Since they were in the past. And that's where it all has to stay. In the past." She took a swallow of wine, handed the bottle back to Kirk and began walking again.

She felt the licking of foamy surf around her ankles and welcomed the cooling effect on her overheated blood.

Kirk had another swallow from the bottle and followed along beside her, humming softly. After a while, he observed, "You're getting the hem of your dress wet."

"You're crowding me into the water."

"Just walking beside you."

"Well, you're walking too close."

He chuckled.

"What are you laughing about?"

"Just remembering that time we went skinny-dipping in the moonlight on that beach near Acapulco. Remember?"

She remembered all too well. The vision of their wet slick bodies gleaming in the moonlight seared across her mind in a flash that made her pulse hammer.

"Want to do it again?"

"Certainly not!"

"Dare you."

"No."

"Then have another drink. We might as well kill the bottle."

She took a swallow of the wine. Then Kirk drained

the last golden liquid from the bottle and carefully placed it on the beach. "I'll pick that up in the morning."

He turned to her.

She backed away from him, deeper into the water that was now swirling around her knees.

"Kirk, leave me alone," she said unsteadily.

"You don't really mean that," he said softly.

"Yes I do!"

"Hey, watch out!"

She had taken another step back. Suddenly a breaker, stronger than expected, caught her behind the knees. She screamed as she went sprawling into the water, arms and legs flailing the air. Then with a splash she was totally engulfed.

Strong arms encircled her, bringing her, spluttering, out of the water.

They were both soaked to the skin, which didn't appear to bother Kirk in the slightest. He was holding her lightly, grinning down at her. Her wet body was plastered against his strong, muscular chest.

"Put me down!" she gasped.

"Sure," he said and stood her on her feet.

They were waist deep in the water. His arms were still around her. Her dress had become no more than a wet film over her bare skin. Kirk's arms tightened, pulling her even closer. Her flimsy, wet clothing gave her no protection from the burning contact of their bodies.

They were on a deserted strip of the beach, alone and secluded here.

Kirk's smoldering gaze drained the strength from

her. His strong thigh forced its way between her legs, then his legs squeezed her thigh in a tight embrace. His wet mouth came down on hers. The kiss burned from her mouth to the depths of her being. Her eyes were closed. Her mind swam; her senses reeled. When the demanding pressure of his lips eased, she gasped his name thickly.

Quickly, with practiced skill, his fingers opened zippers, slipped garments from her shoulders. Her dress floated away in the surf. It was followed by his shirt, his trousers.

Then not even wet clothing separated them. The contact of his naked body against hers was electrifying. Sensations she had not felt in two years exploded within her. Her arms clung to him with desperate hunger. Her legs went around his thighs. Her breath rasped in her throat. They kissed like that, standing in the surf. Then Kirk carried her to the beach at the rim of the water. Gently he laid her on the sand, then stretched out beside her. He tenderly pushed her wet hair back from her eyes and cheeks. His kisses formed a trail of fire down her cheeks to her wet shoulders, to her breasts that had become eager and taut.

Then he pressed his cheek against hers, stroking her hair, and whispered, "Stay with me tonight, Natalie, for the good times we had."

Tears were burning her eyes. No, this was not fair! She felt his need for her, so intense he was trembling. But it had nothing to do with love. He had been dealt a dreadful blow today. His morale was at an all-time low ebb. He needed someone to hold onto, to be close, to help him through the long night. He had touched a very deep, basic part of her that responded to being needed. The heat he was arousing in her was all mixed up with compassion, memories, tenderness.

And combined with all that, was her own hunger, dormant and repressed for two years, awakened in a furious conflagration that now consumed her.

They made love on the beach.

Later, Kirk found their wet garments, washed up by the waves. Then he carried her like a child in his strong arms up to the bed in his cabin where they were drenched in moonlight.

Once again her breath strained in her throat as his caresses fanned the glowing coals into renewed fires. She felt his weight pressing her against the mattress. She cried out. Their moving bodies, painted silver by the moonlight, strained to be closer, closer. The world spun around her.

For a while she was in her own universe with Kirk and then brilliant suns exploded around her.

Long hours after Kirk was sleeping peacefully she lay in his arms, gazing at the sky through the window as stars began fading with the approach of dawn.

In the cold aftermath of passion, she made an attempt at rational thought, trying to understand Kirk's motives and her own. Kirk had needed her tonight. She had served a purpose, giving him comfort to keep him from drowning in depression. Getting drunk would probably have served the same purpose, she realized with a wave of angry humiliation and feeling of degradation.

If she agreed to take the lead part in his production, it would only be a way of him using her again. All he really needed her for was to get studio backing. Kirk was utterly ruthless. As far as he was concerned, love had nothing to do with it.

Tonight he'd needed her body for escape into lust. Tomorrow he'd need her signature on the film contract so he could get to do his movie.

Helpless tears trickled down her cheeks. She was the world's worst patsy where Kirk Trammer was concerned. He didn't love her. He never had. He was in love with someone he'd lost long ago—Jacqueline Davis. He was in love with this film production. He was in love with his own ego. Where was there room left for her?

But in spite of all that, she knew with a hopeless feeling of resignation that she was going to accept the part in his film. Perhaps she had known it all along. There was no other way to save the production and to save Kirk's future. For reasons beyond rational control, she had to do that for Kirk. She was motivated by an emotion stronger than logical thinking.

Was she still in love with Kirk? She had tried to convince herself otherwise. She had blamed tonight's surrender on passion. For two years, she had lived a celibate life. Kirk had awakened starved, primitive hungers. She had been vulnerable and he'd known it and had taken advantage of her.

She found a kind of safety in believing that was what happened. It was frightening to think that her feelings went much deeper, that she was actually still in love with Kirk. She had done her best to harden her heart against Kirk, to build a wall around her feelings and to shut him out. But could she be lying to herself? She couldn't bear the thought of Kirk's disappointment. She was willing to make almost any sacrifice to give him his big chance to produce this film that meant so much to him. She must still care for him a great deal to feel this way.

Yes, she was going to call Sam Kasserman tomorrow and tell him she changed her mind and would take the part. But she made herself a fervent vow. There were going to be no more reruns of what had happened here tonight. From now on until the film was completed, their relationship was going to be strictly professional and impersonal.

To make certain of that . . . to be sure she would not again let physical desire for Kirk's lovemaking gain the upper hand and to insure herself against this continuing aftermath of heartbreak, she was going to be strong and end this farce of a marriage once and for all.

Tomorrow she was going to instruct her lawyer to begin divorce proceedings.

Chapter Six

*N*atalie braced herself for a stormy session when she revealed her plans to her agent.

Ira Bevan's reaction ran the gamut from tearful dismay to near apoplectic fury. "I knew it!" the wizened old agent stormed, pacing in agitated circles. "I knew Kirk Trammer and that bunch of USC friends of yours were going to suck you into this thing. I warned you, didn't I? Tell me if I didn't warn you!"

"Yes, you did, Ira." Natalie sighed patiently. She knew from experience there was no point in discussing the matter in rational terms until Ira had finished exploding.

For the next several minutes, Bevans carried on a heated monologue that ranged from disastrous predictions about Natalie's Hollywood career to black threats on the life of Kirk Trammer. Finally spent, he gulped a glass of fizzing antacid and collapsed into his desk chair, mopping his glistening forehead.

"Ira, you shouldn't get so worked up," Natalie said gently. "One of these days you're going to have a stroke."

"Sure, sure. Better I should be dead than see you in this kind of mess," he grumbled.

"It isn't a mess, Ira. *The Last Encounter* is a strong story and Sam Kasserman at Continental Films is willing to back the production if I take the leading female role."

"Sure, Kasserman wants it," Ira muttered. "With Natalie Brooks in it, he could sell it to an audience of penguins. Is he going to let Kirk direct?"

"That's part of the deal."

Ira shook his head. "That I want to see. Kasserman hates Kirk Trammer. Do you know Kirk threw Sam off the set when he was filming *The Two of Us?* I mean literally. It was on a barge tied up in the Hudson River. Sam came nosing around, making suggestions how to handle a scene. Kirk threw him overboard. Sam had to swim to shore. Everybody was laughing. Sam's never forgiven Kirk for that."

"I've heard the story." Natalie nodded.

Ira went on. "The parent corporation in New York hates Kirk even more because of all the money he cost the company. More to the point, David Clawson, head executive of the corporation, hates Sam Kasserman and wants his head—which he'll get if this turns out to be another Kirk Trammer bomb."

"Well, Sam Kasserman must think it will go or he wouldn't take the chance. He didn't get to be the head of the Continental studios by being dumb, Ira."

"Can't you see, Natalie, it hinges on you? Your latest film, the one they just released, *Never Tomorrow,* is going to make the studio a pile of money. Right now your name is on the top of the list over at Continental. Sam knows it. David Clawson knows it. Most of all, Kirk Trammer knows it."

Ira's verbal sword hit the spot that hurt the most, deep in Natalie's heart. She was all too aware that Kirk's sole interest in her was the door she could open for his production. Blinking back tears, she thought it was cruel of Ira to hit below the belt like that.

"Ira, that's between Kirk and me," she said through stiff lips. "Anyway, I've got more than that at stake. We're setting up a production company. Bill and Sally Dentmen will write the script. Ginny Wells is going to handle special effects. Linda Towers will edit. Kirk will produce and direct. I want you to have our lawyers draw up the necessary papers."

Ira shook his head gloomily. "I hate to think where all this is going to lead. You're getting yourself in quicksand, Natalie. You're an actress. Why not stick to what you do so well? Motion picture production is a crapshoot. What if this turns out to be another dud like *The Two of Us?* You could spend a year in preproduction, shooting and editing the thing and then Continental decides not to release it? A year of your career gone down the drain . . ."

A lot more than that, she thought sadly, considering the price she was going to pay in heartache.

But not to do it meant dashing Kirk's hope to make a comeback and she couldn't bear that, either.

She rose. "Well, I've given it all a lot of thought,

Ira, and I've made my decision. Please start to work on the necessary agreements and contracts."

"All right," the agent said with an expression of morose resignation. "But I want to go on record that I warned you against this."

Before the actual preproduction work could begin, there had to be numerous conferences, meetings and legal fencing. There was a period of wrangling between lawyers, agents and studio executives, for a motion picture today is first of all a business deal.

Natalie was well aware of the fact that back in the days when the big studios had total control of the motion picture industry, pictures were turned out in a kind of assembly-line production. Everything was done within the closed circle of the studio complex. Actors and writers were under long-term contract to the studios. The production crews, sound stages, special effects, back lots were all part of the production line from beginning to end. The studio acquired movie rights to a book or an original screenplay, turned it over to its writers, selected a cast from the actors it had under contract or borrowed from another studio, and oversaw the production to its completion. When the films were done, they were distributed to movie-house chains owned by the studios.

The industry began to change in the 1940s when courts ruled against the monopolistic arrangement and divested the studios of their chains of movie houses. Then along came television in the 1950s and Hollywood was never again the same. The studios could no longer afford to keep highly paid stars under long-term contracts. Large back lots became a financial liability. Films were shot more and more on location. Special effects, which had once been one of the studios' departments, were now often handled by independent specialists.

For the most part, picture making had evolved into a one-shot deal. Each motion picture production was an individual project between the studio and producer, director and actors.

In spite of the changes, the major studios were still the main factor in the making of motion pictures. When a deal was struck with a producer the studio might furnish most of the financing. The producer and his crew moved in and used some of the studio's facilities, the sound stages and equipment during the filming of the motion picture. And when it had been edited and was ready for release, it would be the studios who handled distribution. In that area, the studios remained as powerful as ever.

Before real work on the production could begin, the story synopsis had to be expanded into a complete script. "Give us six weeks," Bill Dentmen promised. "We'll burn a lot of midnight oil."

Natalie fled to the East Coast during that time to avoid Kirk. She returned to Hollywood when she got a call from her cousin, Ginny, that the Dentmens had completed the script and a conference to cast the principals had been scheduled.

The meeting was held in Sam Kasserman's office at the Continental studios. When Natalie entered the room that morning she came face-to-face with Kirk for the first time since that night she had slept with him in the Malibu beach house.

The room was filled. The Dentmens were there as were Ginny Wells and Linda Towers; Natalie's agent,

Ira Bevans; and, seated at his throne, the vast mahogany desk, flanked by vice-presidents and lawyers, Sam Kasserman.

Seeing Kirk again was an unnerving experience for Natalie. He moved to her side, his intense, hazel-eyed gaze moving over her with an intimate look that had all of her nerve ends tingling.

"I've been trying to reach you," he said in a low, angry voice.

"I've been out of town," she replied nervously.

"So I gathered." His gaze burned into her like a deadly laser. "Were you in hiding?"

"Why do you ask that?"

"You pulled a pretty good disappearing act. I called your agent, all of your friends. Nobody would tell me where you were."

She shrugged. "I flew East for a few days."

His voice was harsh. "I assumed that. I tried a few calls in that direction with no luck. When you go into seclusion you do a good job of it."

"Why were you trying to reach me?"

He raised an eyebrow, giving her a searching look that made her knees quiver. "I've been advised by your attorney that you've filed for divorce."

She swallowed hard. She had been dreading this moment. Unable to speak, she simply nodded.

Kirk's frown was a dark thundercloud. "Were you that disappointed with our lovemaking on the beach?"

"Kirk, be quiet. Somebody is going to hear you."

"Hear what? That I made love to my own wife?" He smiled bitterly. "Maybe that would create a scandal in today's society. Anyway, I cannot understand why you would file for divorce and pull a disappearing act after that night. It was like a regular second honeymoon, don't you agree?"

Her face was burning. His words awoke the memory of that night of passion, sending a flash of heat through her body. She suddenly became aware of the fabric of her dress brushing her thighs, the tightening of her nipples against a bra that suddenly seemed too small. She swallowed hard, trying to quiet the hurried tempo of her pulse. When she replied, her voice was thick, betraying the churning emotions he had aroused in her. "Kirk, shut up. This is a business meeting."

She turned away from him abruptly, walking over to greet her friends and her agent.

Then Kasserman took control of the meeting, saying, "All right, let's see if we can put this thing together."

By now the Dentmens had delivered the completed script. Numerous photocopies had been made, bound, and sent around to various departments. Department heads were breaking the pages down into sets and props and travel costs. It was obvious that the studio intended to keep extremely close tabs on this production.

Now it was time for the creative people to find actors for the principal roles in the cast. It was firmly established and agreed by all concerned that Natalie would play the part of Rebecca Abrahms, the Israeli news correspondent.

The other two major roles, Clay Winters, the space

scientist hero-protagonist and Nichole Nikova, the beautiful Russian agent, had to be selected. Also an actor had to be chosen to play the role of Komen Assarat, the villain, the story menace who had taken control of an oil rich Mideastern country and developed the capability of destroying the protective space station. Another important role was that of Clay Winters's boss and mentor, the head scientist of the space program, a dignified older man named Jerome Ambers.

Kirk, with his customary, brash self-assurance immediately took the floor. "Since I've been carrying this story around in my mind for months, I can see the part of Clay Winters clearly. I want Jerry Rhodes in the part."

"Rhodes?" Kasserman exclaimed incredulously. "I hope you're not serious."

"Of course I'm serious!" Kirk said, bristling. "I know my own story. Rhodes would be terrific in the role."

"What do you mean, terrific? The guy is a nobody. Whoever heard of him except a few avant-garde movie buffs? Listen, this is an expensive picture. I can't put a nobody in the lead role."

The meeting had just begun and already Kirk and Kasserman were close to yelling at each other.

Natalie gazed at the two men. The air fairly crackled with the electrified clash of two powerful personalities.

Behind his desk, Kasserman was the image of imperious self-assurance. His mane of wavy silver hair was a contrast to the deep country club tan, his costly grooming, tailored gray suit, imported shoes, heavy gold bracelet. It all gave him a regal air, the look of an executive who wielded tremendous power.

Natalie thought that Kasserman's blood red silk necktie probably cost more than Kirk's entire wardrobe. As usual, Kirk wore scuffed Western boots, a sport shirt, a rumpled leather jacket. His mop of bushy, dark hair looked uncombed. But he had a lanky, rangy physical strength like a coiled lariat that had a primitive energy force equal in every respect to Kasserman.

For her part, seeing Kirk in action awakened an inner heat like coals being fanned. She couldn't drag her gaze from him. The blazing intensity in his eyes sent an electric charge down her spine.

Against her will, Natalie responded to the power of his dynamic personality as much as to his physical appeal. She was aware of the quickened rush of blood through her temples. Everyone in the Continental studios complex from vice-presidents down to janitors were intimidated and awed by the all-powerful studio head, Sam Kasserman. Not so Kirk Trammer. If anything, there was an element of disdain in Kirk's attitude as if, being totally confident of his own artistic and creative ability, he held the studio head somewhat in contempt.

In spite of her anger at Kirk, in this moment, she felt a rush of admiration for the way he dared stand up to the omnipotent studio head. She thought with a feeling of despair that Kirk was the most dynamic, attractive man she had ever met. He was exciting in a way that overwhelmed her. *What is this power he has over me?* she asked herself hopelessly. If they were alone right this minute and he asked her to go to bed with him, she wouldn't know how she could find the strength to turn him down.

"Jerry Rhodes has talent. He's going to be very big one of these days," Kirk said evenly, his gaze leveled like a double-barrel shotgun at Kasserman's head.

"He might be big one day," Kasserman shot back. "Right now he's a nobody."

There was a moment of steaming silence. The Dentmens, Ginny Wells and Linda Towers looked upset. Kirk had convinced them that Jerry Rhodes would be ideal for the part.

Kirk began again. "The point is, my production group has discussed this. We love Rhodes for the part and I've as good as told him he can have it."

"I'm sorry. You'll have to tell him there's been a change. You can't use him."

"What do you mean by that?" Kirk said, his voice sounding dangerous. "According to the deal we made with you, I can make that kind of decision."

"I don't care anything about any kind of deal," Kasserman said, his voice rising. "I am not going to make a picture this costly with a nobody like Jerry Rhodes in the lead role and that's final."

Kirk again lapsed into fuming silence. He looked at his lawyer, who shrugged and made a hopeless gesture with upturned palms.

So much for any contractual agreements Kirk might have made with the studio, Natalie thought with a wave of sympathy for her embattled husband. In a showdown, Kasserman would choose to fight a contractual lawsuit rather than give in on a major point. With the legal and financial resources of a vast corporation complex behind him, he knew he had little to fear from Kirk, who was broke to begin with.

The studio head broke the fuming silence. "I've picked your lead. I want Tom Sacks in the part. I've talked to Tom. He's read the script. He likes it. I've made him an offer and I think he'll take it."

There was an audible murmur around the room. Like the others, Natalie reacted with surprise. Tom Sacks was certainly big enough. He was the macho hero in every woman's fantasy life. It was surprising that he would agree to do the picture. He had to be swamped with offers. Natalie had to give Kasserman credit—he swung a lot of influence around Hollywood. At the same time, she thought a lot of the budget would go to Tom Sacks. He could demand and get plenty.

Kirk reacted with a dark frown. "Sacks is an egotistical ham. He's going to demand all kinds of special treatment. We'll have to sacrifice shooting time to pay what he'll want. And he'll try to take over every scene he's in."

Kasserman gave Kirk a baleful look. "I'll match your ego against Tom Sacks's any day. With you directing, I don't think we'll have to worry about anybody else taking over anything."

"Well," Kirk added, "I guess he's not the worst actor in town, though he certainly wouldn't have been my first choice for the part." He swung his gaze to Natalie. "How do you feel about acting opposite Tom Sacks, hon?"

Natalie shrugged. "I can work with him. I think he'll be all right for the part. And as Sam says, his ego is no bigger than yours."

A ripple of nervous laughter ran around the room.

Kirk's lips moved in a wry, sardonic grin. "Touché." Then he said, "I'll compromise, Sam. If I have to take Tom Sacks in the role of the protagonist, then I want Mark Landers to play the heavy, the Middle-Eastern dictator."

Kasserman scowled, then nodded slowly. "All right."

"And for the part of Jerome Ambers, I want Sir David George."

There was an audible intake of breath around the room. Kasserman's eyebrows elevated at the name of the eminent British actor. He grunted. "You don't want much, do you?"

"Well, you said you wanted some big names. The part of Jerome Ambers is important. It demands an actor with an air of reserve and dignity. At least Sir George is a real actor, not a ham like Tom Sacks who gets by on his macho image."

Kasserman drummed on his desk. There was a heavy silence. Natalie suspected he was struggling with a mental conflict over the cost the award-winning British actor could demand and the stature his name would add to the film. Finally, he said, "All right, if you think you can afford both Tom Sacks and Sir David George and still bring this thing in under budget."

"Sure," Kirk said confidently.

Natalie was both amused and exasperated by Kirk's cocksure attitude. He wasn't the slightest bit intimidated by Sam Kasserman. She doubted if he'd be intimidated by the devil, himself!

Kasserman nodded. "Good, then that's settled.

Now how about the other female role, the Russian girl."

"I have her picked out, too," Kirk said. "I'd like to see Marsha Sanders in the part."

It was Natalie's turn to be shocked and furious. She felt stunned, unable to believe that her ears were not playing tricks. Surely Kirk couldn't be so utterly callous and inconsiderate as to humiliate her in this way—bringing the woman he had been linked with in all the scandal rags into the same picture with Natalie! It took all her effort to swallow a sudden rush of angry tears.

Kasserman plucked at his lower lip thoughtfully. "She's dark, she's beautiful—looks Russian. Not all that well known. But with names like Tom Sacks and Natalie Brooks on the marquee, to say nothing of Sir David George, that won't be too much of a problem. She had the lead in that turkey of yours, *The Two of Us,* but that wasn't her fault. Maybe by now the public will forgive her—"

"In Europe—" Kirk began heatedly.

Kasserman held up a hand wearily. "Please spare me. Don't tell me about Europe. Okay, Marsha Sanders. If she'll take the part, you've got her."

Natalie felt smothered by a wave of heart-wrenching despair mixed with impotent rage. How could she possibly spend weeks, perhaps months acting before the camera with a woman who'd had an affair with her husband? And how could she know the affair was over? Obviously it was not or Kirk wouldn't be so dead set on having Marsha in the picture. There were plenty of other competent actresses available, many of them with more screen credits. But none who bore the incredible resemblance to his dead sweet-heart, Natalie reminded herself with a wrenching pang.

The meeting ended. Natalie gathered up her purse and walked quickly to the door. A hand caught her arm. She spun around to face Kirk. Her eyes flashed angrily.

"What's your hurry?" Kirk asked.

"I have things to do," she said coldly.

"I want to talk to you. Have lunch with me."

"No."

"Why not?"

"I have other plans."

"Break them."

She gasped, eyes widening. "Where do you get off giving me orders like that, Kirk Trammer?"

He considered the question, his dark-eyed gaze burning into her like a hot torch. "As your husband, I might not have that authority," he said mildly. "These days they have laws against a husband using force with a rebellious wife. However, as your director, I am ordering you to have lunch with me. It's a matter of business."

Her eyes narrowed. "Very well. Strictly business."

His firm hand grasping her arm led her from the office building across the studio grounds to a lunchroom where Kirk seated her in a secluded booth. He ordered a light lunch, then pinned her again with his penetrating gaze.

"I want an explanation," he began.

"What do you mean?"

"You know good and well what I mean! I want answers to the questions I asked you before the meeting. Why did you pull the disappearing act after that night in Malibu?"

Natalie felt a fresh wave of anger. "You said you brought me here to discuss business."

"We'll get to that later."

She started to rise, but he grasped her wrist firmly and sat her back down.

"Kirk, how dare you—" she said in a low, furious voice.

A taunting smile tugged at his lips. "Shall we have a family row in public? That should make juicy material for the scandal sheets."

Natalie felt smothered by impotent rage. It was true that gossipmongers were everywhere, ever eager to pounce on a movie celebrity's personal life. Kirk had her trapped here.

"Well?" he asked.

"Kirk, I told you there wasn't going to be a repeat of what happened that night. I want a divorce."

His brows drew together. Anger was sharp in his eyes. She felt a cold, deep chasm widening between them. It sent a shiver down her spine.

"Very well," he said coldly. "But you're not getting out of here until you give me an explanation. That night on the beach and in the cabin, you wanted me as much as I wanted you. You can't make me believe you didn't get a thrill out of making love with me."

Her cheeks flamed. "All right, I won't deny it. You've been gone for two years. I was vulnerable— starved for some lovemaking."

"Not with just any man, though," he insisted, his gaze boring into her.

"That's true. Sex with you has always been special.

I'll admit that. But there has to be more to marriage than lust. And we don't have more than that. I want out, Kirk."

"All right, if that's what you want," he said with cold fury. "I don't go chasing after any woman!"

Except Marsha Sanders, Natalie thought bitterly. Then she corrected herself. It was actually the ghost of his real love, Jacqueline Davis, the only woman he'd ever loved, come alive in her living counterpart.

She wondered if Kirk was really aware of the true nature of his attraction for Marsha? Was it a subtle, unconscious thing, a searching to fulfill a longing that had been denied him? Whatever it was, he was completely under its power. There was no room left for Natalie.

The lunch became a strained, impersonal matter. Kirk t   alked about the picture, his plans for flying the cast and the camera crew to Rio to begin filming that phase of the production while Ginny Wells and her special effects crew began work on the space station sets.

As for Natalie, she made perfunctory replies, poking at her untouched food, unable to swallow past the hurting lump in her throat. She was enormously relieved when Kirk paid the bill and she could escape his presence.

Before leaving for Rio, Natalie paid a visit to Special Effects Unlimited, Inc., where her cousin, Ginny, and her crew of experts were tackling the problems of visual effects that would be seen in *The Last Encounter*.

Several weeks had passed and the preproduction

work had been underway. Casting, budgeting, props, set design, costuming, and location scouting were matters that had to be taken care of before a foot of film could be shot. A whole army of people had been hired: art director; set designer; costume designer; wardrobe masters and wardrobe mistresses; the property master who was the custodian of the props; specialists in various fields such as electricians; camera crews; stuntmen and stuntwomen; makeup people and hairdressers and the grips—the handymen who handled the chores of moving things around for various camera setups. It was the grips who made difficult camera angles possible by building scaffolds for camera crews or setting up tracks along which camera dollies could move.

Already, storyboards portraying major scenes in the film had been sketched and painted by artists and were arranged along a wall.

Despite her emotional turmoil over her pending divorce, Natalie couldn't help feeling a wave of excitement as the movie production got underway. Seeing the artists' projection of the major scenes brought the movie more alive than just reading the script. She exclaimed over the dramatic scenes in outer space, the colorful episodes in romantic Rio and the suspenseful action sequences in the strife torn Middle East.

Natalie pointed to a sketch showing astronauts flying around the space station in their self-propelled space suits. The background was the black velvet of the universe sprinkled with diamonds of distant planets.

"You special effects experts never cease to amaze me," Natalie said, shaking her head in wonder. "How are you going to pull that off?"

"Simple if you know how." Ginny shrugged.

"Having people fly around in the air is simple?"

"Often we do stunts like that with piano wire. We'll design the space suits, put stunt guys in them and hang them from scaffolds with piano wire. That's how a lot of flying sequences, cars dangling over the edge of cliffs, stuff like that, are done. Piano wire is extremely strong, but very thin and invisible when filmed against the right background. After shooting the space men suspended in midair, we'll use rear-screen and front-screen projection techniques as well as matte and traveling matte processes to make it look like they're in the outer space setting."

Ginny showed Natalie some models of the space station and shuttle. "Miniaturization," she explained. "On the screen they'll look full size. The original King Kong was a brainchild of the pioneer animator, Willis H. O'Brien. Y'know, King Kong was actually a clay model eighteen inches high. He was made to move by using stop frame photography, that is, shooting one frame at a time, while adjusting the figure to move slightly with each advancing frame. It's the same principal in cartoon-type animation, except there the figures are drawn. When the completed frames are run through the projector at normal speed you get the effect of fluid motion."

"Takes a lot of time," Natalie observed.

"Yes, and patience, although our modern setups use a type of camera synchronization that speeds it up."

She pointed to the artist sketches of Middle-Eastern desert and village scenes. "This is going to be tough and expensive. Kirk wants to build full-size sets of buildings and streets for battle scenes, shelling, fires. I have to come up with armored vehicles and tanks, no less. Then there are the robot-controlled space craft developed by the power hungry Middle-Eastern dictator, the battle scenes in space between our space shuttle craft and the attacking rockets." She shook her head. "This is expensive stuff, Natalie. And Kirk is so darn demanding. He'd think nothing of tossing months of work out the window if it doesn't satisfy him."

Natalie frowned. "Ginny, is he going to be able to stay within the budget on this film?"

"Frankly, I doubt it. Not with the kinds of things he wants to do. You know Kirk."

"I think we're going to be in for a lot of problems with the studio," Natalie murmured.

"You know they're insisting on naming their own associate producer. Kasserman wants Howard Ansco."

"Good Lord, Kirk hates him."

"I think the feeling is mutual."

"Ansco will be sniffing around every move Kirk makes, and reporting back to the studio."

"We'll be lucky if the battle scenes are only in the film. So you're off to Rio next week."

Natalie nodded.

"Lucky you. While we're slaving away on these sets you'll be soaking up South American sunshine, living it up in Rio." Ginny grinned. "You ought to get plenty of inspiration to play the love scenes. Rio is one of the most romantic cities in the world. And you'll be there during the carnival season. I should have taken up acting instead of special effects!"

"Lucky?" Natalie asked. "I'm not sure about that, Ginny."

Her cousin touched her arm, her eyes filling with sympathy. "I know it's going to be tough on you, Natalie, working with Kirk every day while going through the strain of a divorce. I—I wish there were something I could do to help."

Natalie shook her head. "I don't guess there's anything anyone can do to make a divorce painless."

"I wish it hadn't come to this. We were all hoping that you and Kirk—"

"I know. But it's a hopeless situation, Ginny. I can't go on being married to a man who doesn't love me, whose only interest in me is using me to realize his ambition. When this film is finished, when Kirk gets what he wants, he'll have no further use for me. He'll take off for Europe again, probably with Marsha Sanders. I'm just beating him to the draw. It hurts now, but in the long run, I'm going to save myself even worse heartbreak. When we get this film done and my divorce is final, maybe I can pick up the pieces and start over with a new life."

Natalie thought it was going to be a real test of her acting ability to play love scenes with another man while her husband, Kirk, the only man she had ever loved, whom she was now putting out of her life, would be watching every move. And to make the strain even greater, the actress Kirk was involved with, Marsha Sanders, would be in many of the scenes, too.

She doubted if the scenes in front of the camera were going to be half as dramatic as the real-life situation going on behind the cameras.

Chapter Seven

*R*io De Janeiro . . .

High above the city of Rio de Janeiro, on the peak of Mount Corcovado, shrouded in clouds and mists, stood the magnificent figure of Christ the Redeemer, arms outstretched, as if in benediction for the world below. Across Botafogo Bay the rounded peak of Sugar Loaf Mountain posed like a sentinel looking out to sea.

The grandeur of the setting dissolved into the reality of a small crowded street where sweating camera crews waited impatiently as makeup people rushed in to make hasty repairs to the actors wearily preparing to do the seventh take of the same scene.

On a crane high above their heads, the film director, Kirk Trammer, shouted instructions to the technicians.

Natalie felt like a broiled potato in the scorching

sun of Rio's February midsummer day. She tried to be patient as her makeup lady did her job.

Natalie was a professional. Long, weary hours repeating take after take in uncomfortable and sometimes dangerous situations were part of her job. One day, months from now, an audience would sit in the air-conditioned comfort of a movie theater and be transported into a fantasy world of romance and adventure on the screen. Right now it was difficult to reconcile that make-believe story with the reality of glaring sun, dusty streets, tired muscles and strained emotions. Working under a demanding perfectionist, whom it was next to impossible to satisfy, did not make matters any easier.

"Ready, people, this is a take," called the assistant director. "Cameras—action."

One of the technicians stepped before the cameras and snapped his blackboard marker with the scene and take number scribbled on it.

Natalie took a breath and shed the personality of Natalie Brooks. In an instant, a flickering of an eye, something inside her clicked and she was transformed into another human being—Rebecca Abrahms. It was more than playacting. She *was* Rebecca Abrahms. She knew the bitter sorrow of seeing parents killed in a bombing raid. She suffered the uncertain agony of a husband known only a short while before being captured and not certain now if he were dead or alive in a prison camp.

She knew terror . . . the terror of being caught up in a life-threatening situation, but one from which she could not escape. It was sweeping her in a rushing torrent into a situation that could decide the fate of the world.

Now she was in the small side street in Rio, tensely pretending to shop the wares of street vendors as she waited for the contact that could lead her to the heart of the dark, international plot.

Suddenly she caught sight of a man moving toward her through the crowd. Her eyes widened with surprise and dismay. It was not the contact she was expecting. It was a familiar figure in a rumpled seersucker suit, looking very American in this Brazilian crowd. It was Clay Winters, the space scientist she had met on her trip to the American space station. There had been a dangerous attraction between them from the first instant. She had fought it, reminding herself of her husband, who might still be alive.

What was Clay Winters doing here? What folly had caused the stubborn man to follow her? It was sheer insanity. There was no place in her life at this complicated moment for Clay Winters!

She tried to lose herself in the crowd. But he caught up with her in a few quick strides.

"Rebecca!"

She spun around, stared up at him with stricken eyes. "Clay—what are you doing here?"

"I followed you, of course. I couldn't just let you walk out of my life."

"But you must! This is insanity."

She looked around like a trapped creature. What if she were seen talking to an American so closely tied to the space program? It would spoil everything. And it would put him in the kind of danger she was in.

But his hands were gripping her arms. He looked down at her intently. "I found out you were coming to Rio. I caught the first plane. I had a devil of a time finding you. Now that I have, I'm not going to let you go."

Her tear-filled eyes pleaded with him. "You must, Clay. You have to forget about me. There are things about me you don't understand."

"I understand I never felt this way about a woman before in my life. You feel it too. Don't lie. I can see it in your eyes, Rebecca!"

"Please . . ." Her conflict was becoming unbearable.

Then—

"Cut!" Kirk called wearily.

Natalie felt an unpleasant shock. For a moment she was a sleepwalker coming out of a dream, a subject jerked rudely out of a hypnotic trance. She drew the back of her hands across her eyes, shaking off that other world, coming back to the world of Natalie Brooks.

"Kirk, what is it now?" she demanded.

Kirk, riding the chair of the boom, swung down to their level. He was glaring at Tom Sacks. Natalie could see he was making a superhuman effort to get his temper under control.

"Tom," he said with remarkable constraint, "I have to remind you again that in the role of Clay Winters, you are the intellectual type. A space scientist. This is something quite out of character for you—to go chasing thousands of miles after a woman you met briefly. You are confused, troubled, out of your environment, but in the grip of an obsession that has overridden your normal restraint and inhibitions. You are not Burt Reynolds wisecracking your way through a hot rod race. You are not Harrison Ford playing the dashing Indiana Jones. You are not Tom Selleck wowing the ladies with one glance. Do you think for this once you could submerge all that self-confident macho charm that seems to ooze out of you like sweat on a hot day and pull this off with a bit more finesse?"

For a moment there was no reply. Sacks and Trammer dueled with their eyes. "I heard you were a horse's south end on the set," Sacks said slowly. "I took this part because Sam Kasserman twisted my arm. I'm beginning to regret it."

"Well, he twisted my arm, too. But like it or not, we're in this together. I'm not trying to win any popularity contests on the set. I have only one goal— and that is to make one heck of a good motion picture. Now we can either keep shooting this scene over for the next five days, or we can get it right the next time and go home for the day. It's up to you."

"By 'right' you mean the way you want it," Sacks muttered.

"Exactly," Kirk nodded.

There was another moment of tension, then Sacks shrugged and walked back to the position he took at the beginning of the scene.

Kirk turned to Natalie. He was still frowning. "Natalie, there's something wrong with the way you are playing Rebecca Abrahms."

Her eyes widened. For a moment she was speechless. Then she bristled. "What do you mean by that?"

"Well, I think you're having trouble shifting gears from the kind of roles you've been playing. The producers, writers and directors you've been working with have been playing up the Grace Kelly image because you look so much like her and have the same kind of poised, cool polish. That's been fine for the sophisticated, suburban temptress roles you've had on TV and the films you've done. But Rebecca Abrahms is an entirely different woman. There's an earthy element in this character. She grew up working in the soil with her family, coaxing plants out of the desert soil of Israel with her bare hands. She didn't attend a sheltered finishing school the way you did. She has the physical constitution of farming people. She sweats in the sun and her hair gets scraggly, and still with all of that, she manages to look sexy and convey her femininity."

"I know all that," Natalie said abruptly. "I read the script."

"Did you?"

"What kind of a sarcastic crack is that?"

"I didn't mean it as sarcasm," Kirk replied. "What I meant was when you were reading the script, did you really see Rebecca Abrahms the way I'm describing her?"

"Kirk, you may have the reputation of some kind of boy genius hotshot director. But I'm a professional actress. While you were sulking over in Europe, I made a TV special and several movies, all of them successful. I know what I'm doing."

"I didn't say you were an amateur. I respect your ability. You're getting across the emotion of tension and fear just fine. It's the core of the character you're playing that I'm concerned about. I don't think you've yet grasped fully the deeper facets of the character of Rebecca Abrahms. The critics are going to sense that and call your portrayal shallow. I want you to give some thought to what I've said."

With that, he abruptly turned away, leaving Natalie standing there, fuming with humiliation and rage.

Kirk nodded to his assistant director.

"Ready! Places everybody," the A.D. bawled. "All right, camera one, camera two, camera three. Roll 'em. Action!"

"At least the weather is cooperating," Kirk said gloomily.

"What do you expect?" Toby Calkins muttered. "Rio de Janeiro in February. The middle of summer down here. There's supposed to be a lot of sunshine." He took out a handkerchief and mopped his round, florid features even though they were in the comparative comfort of an air-conditioned restaurant.

It was the following evening. Kirk had announced a twenty-four hour break in the filming schedule as they prepared for the big Mardi Gras carnival scenes. He had assembled the principal members of the cast and some key production people for a dinner meeting. He had reserved the hotel dining room where a banquet-length table had been set up.

They had just come from the building rented by the production company where a screening room had been set up. For the last hour they had been viewing rushes of the scenes shot the day before.

The reason for Kirk's dark mood was obvious to Natalie. After a dozen takes they still had not done the street scene to his satisfaction.

Kirk was seated at the head of the table. On his right was Toby Calkins, who was the director of photography. The other members of the cast were seated around the long table.

Natalie viewed the scene from her place at the lower end of the table. She had deliberately chosen a seat as far away from Kirk as possible. She was still furious with him for humiliating her in front of the cast and camera crew yesterday. However, in spite of her anger, she couldn't escape her awareness of how Kirk's dynamic personality could utterly dominate a gathering, even one comprising the powerful egos assembled here today.

Her gaze strayed from Kirk to the others. She glanced at Tom Sacks; then her gaze shifted from Sacks to the actress across the table from him. She felt a rush of hot blood to her cheeks. Looking at Marsha Sanders, Natalie was aware of mingled hurt and anger twisting inside her, cutting like the sharp edge of a knife.

She had to admit that Marsha was perfect in the role of the female Soviet agent. With her dark hair and huge, dark eyes, she looked like a daughter of Russia. She was a perfect contrast to Natalie's fair features.

Natalie managed to keep her hurt and tears hidden. Her pride refused to let Kirk see her make a jealous scene over the matter of hiring Marsha for the film. It was just one more rift in the widening chasm between her and Kirk. She thought either Kirk was totally blind to her feelings or was so wrapped up in Marsha that he had to have her close during the shooting of this film.

Looking at her now, Natalie could understand why Kirk had become involved with Marsha. Her resemblance to his dead sweetheart, Jacqueline Davis, was uncanny. It was as if the beautiful singer had returned from the grave and walked back into Kirk's life. How could Natalie hope to compete with something like that?

Kirk spent the dinner hour going over his plans for the Carnival scenes. "By the way, we've run into a bit of luck," he said at one point. "I happened to meet a rich American who is vacationing down here on his yacht. He's a big movie fan. Offered to rent us his luxury yacht for some filming at a ridiculously low price. Bill, can you write a yacht scene into the script? It would make a great setting, the yacht riding in the harbor with Rio in the background."

Bill Dentmen frowned. "How in the heck are we going to tie that into the story at this point, Kirk?"

"That's your problem, Bill. You're the writer. I'm sure you can come up with something plausible."

There was a lively discussion about the added scenes. Finally, the meeting broke up.

Natalie watched the others mingle and drift toward the exit. Marsha Sanders had moved to Kirk's side. They became engrossed in a private conversation. Then Marsha linked her arm through Kirk's with a possessive gesture. Still talking, they strolled through the lobby and walked out into the night together. Natalie stared at the two of them, boiling with fury. Marsha had deliberately made a point of letting the whole production company know that she had something special going with Kirk.

Through a blur of angry tears, Natalie found the elevator button. In her room, she picked up a book and hurled it at a wall, wishing with all her heart that Kirk were the target.

Chapter Eight

$\mathcal{K}$irk felt the heat of the day lingering oppressively in the night air. It matched the weight of responsibility that rested heavily on his shoulders.

"You look worried and tense, Kirk," Marsha commented.

"That goes with the territory, starting a major film, as you well know, Marsha."

She squeezed his arm. "You need a minute to relax. How about a nightcap before turning in? I found a neat little cocktail lounge a couple of blocks from here. Besides, I have some things I want to talk with you about."

"What things?"

She winked mysteriously. "Tell you over our drinks."

They found a secluded table in a quiet corner. The lights were dim, the Latin tempo of the small music combo soft and unobtrusive. The waiter brought tropical drinks in tall, frosted glasses. Kirk sipped his drink and gazed at his companion. Marsha was a remarkably beautiful woman. Her raven hair and enormous dark eyes contrasted with a flawless, creamy complexion that she protected from the sun. Any man would enjoy looking at her.

Kirk enjoyed Marsha's company. He felt relaxed with her. If any other member of the cast had brought him here, he would be on guard, braced for verbal fencing over some new demand or complaint. But Marsha was easy to get along with. She was a competent actress who did her job well and seldom made waves.

Kirk broke several minutes of companionable silence. "Did you really have something mysterious to discuss with me or did you kidnap me under false pretenses?"

She laughed softly. "No big mystery, Kirk. I guess I saw a chance to steal you for a half hour and grabbed it. I haven't seen you since we finished filming *The Two of Us.*"

"You've seen me every day since we started production on *The Last Encounter.*"

"Oh, sure. On the set with dozens of people around. I mean like this." She waved her hand at the quiet, secluded surroundings. "A few minutes by ourselves, just to talk."

"Yeah, things have been hectic," Kirk admitted. "I don't guess I've been by myself for five minutes since production got underway."

Marsha toyed with her glass. "I haven't had the

chance to thank you for getting me this part, Kirk. I know you asked for me."

"No thanks needed. You're perfect for the part. It was just good casting."

"Come on," she chided gently. "You know there are a dozen competent actresses around who could play Nichole Nikova."

"Maybe. I wanted you."

She raised her eyes, giving him a searching look. "Why?"

"Why?"

"Yes, why?" she persisted, her gaze unwavering.

"Because I worked with you in *The Two of Us.* I thought you did a fantastic job in the part. I'm familiar with your style and I know you take direction well."

She chewed her bottom lip thoughtfully. "I wondered if it was because you thought you owed me."

"Owed you?"

"Yes. *The Two of Us* turned out to be such a box office disaster. Maybe you thought it hurt my career."

"I did worry some about that, Marsha. It wasn't fair to you. You know the public. Sometimes they associate an actor or actress with a film that bombs out. That was your first major role. It wasn't the best thing that could have happened to your career. I would like to make that up to you if I can."

There was a moment of silence. She touched her tongue to her lips. "I—I was hoping maybe it might be more personal than that."

Kirk looked at her thoughtfully. "Care to explain that statement?"

"Oh, Kirk, you know darn good and well what I mean," she said chidingly. "I never have made a secret of how I feel about you." She laughed self-consciously. "Remember those ridiculous tabloid stories that linked us in a torrid love affair during the filming of *The Two of Us?* I often wished they were true."

"Marsha—"

But she interrupted. "Kirk, you don't have to say anything. I know you're still too much in love with Natalie to look at another woman. But I just had to let you know that I still feel the same about you. If . . . well, if things between you and Natalie fall through, I'm waiting in the wings to grab you." She blushed. "Sorry if that makes me sound like an aggressive female, but at this stage of the game, I can't see any advantage in being coy."

Kirk smiled ruefully. "Right now, Marsha, I wouldn't give a whole lot of odds for Natalie and me getting back together. She's filed for divorce, you know."

"Yes, I heard that. But it doesn't change a whole lot, does it? I mean, you're still in love with her. . . ."

It was half a statement, half a question.

Kirk sighed. "That doesn't help very much. Marsha, I really have dealt Natalie a lot of misery. I can't blame her for wanting to get me out of her life."

"You mean, going off to Europe for two years?"

"Well, that and some other things."

Kirk felt compelled to talk. Was it because he'd kept his feelings under tight wraps for so long? Was it because he'd always been a loner? He had few friends, none of them very close . . . none he could talk with about his true, inner feelings. Once he'd had a very close buddy with whom he could share his feelings, and that friend had been killed in Viet Nam. Then there had been Jacqueline, the vibrant, compelling girl who had shared his innermost dreams and thoughts, and she had died in the tragic accident. After that, he had kept a wall around his personal life.

Now in this quiet setting, his defenses lowered by the drink, he surprised himself by verbalizing personal heartaches that he normally kept bottled up. "Natalie has accused me of marrying her when I was still in love with a girl in my past."

"I know," Marsha said with a slow nod. "I played her part in *The Two of Us.*" Her lips moved in a wry smile. "It gave me a spooky feeling, like I was a ghost or something. I knew you were trying to bring her alive through me. They say I look a lot like her."

"You do. I guess it's no secret in the trade or among people involved in that production that it was a chapter out of my past. I think I had to do that film, Marsha. It was a way of living it all over. In those scenes where you sang those wild rock numbers with the lights flashing and the band hard and driving behind you, and you tossing your head back, swinging your body to the music . . . yes, it was Jacqueline come alive again, for sure. But it wasn't something I wanted to hold onto. It was a catharsis. In the film, I brought Jacqueline back to life and gave her the moment of success she dreamed about but didn't live to see. I went through all of it again with her. When it was over and I saw the finished, edited job on the screen, I knew at last I had put the ghost of Jacqueline Davis to rest."

Kirk felt a damp film of perspiration bead his forehead. He paused to take a drink from his glass.

"Small wonder the critics liked *The Two of Us*," Marsha murmured. "You wrenched it right out of your soul."

"The Europeans saw what I was doing. It was the biggest thing at the film festival in Cannes that year," Kirk agreed. "But the box office appeal was zilch. In the eyes of the industry I was a failure. That was why I had to get out of Natalie's life. In my own eyes I was a failure. And her career was taking off like a skyrocket. I was hanging around the house, living off her income." He shook his head. "The situation was impossible. But when I was in Europe, I got some self-respect back. I got a clear vision of my own feelings. I realized Natalie had been right. The memory of Jacqueline was haunting me so it kept coming between us. Now I'd cleared that up. And then I started getting the idea for *The Last Encounter*. Just like I'd done *The Two of Us* for Jacqueline's memory, I knew *The Last Encounter* was going to be Natalie's film."

Marsha blinked back tears. "So what's the big problem between the two of you, now?" she asked bitterly. "Sounds like all your problems have been cleared up. Why don't you fight the divorce? Grab her up in your arms, tell her what you've just told me. If she cares anything about you, she'll cancel the stupid divorce."

"It isn't that simple," Kirk muttered.

He lapsed into moody silence, wrestling with his own thoughts. The basic situation hadn't changed. Natalie was even a bigger star now than when he left for Europe. Her career was a huge success. He was still a failure, trying to make a comeback. Natalie thought he was using her to get to do this film. In a crazy, ironic way, she was partly right. Kirk thought, almost desperately, that he had to do this film if he was going to save himself and, in the process, save their marriage. The only way he was able to get the studio backing was if Natalie agreed to play the lead role, so he'd made that compromise, hoping the end would justify the means. Had he done the right thing? If he could get the film completed there was no question in his mind that it was going to be a box office smash hit, one of the biggest money-makers of the season. Then he could hold his head high again.

The last thing he wanted from Natalie was pity. That night in Malibu when they had made love after the two years' absence, he now realized she'd given in out of pity. She'd brought the news of the studio turndown of his production. He'd been crushed. That had set the stage for what happened that night. Natalie was compassionate, bighearted, an easy touch. She had wanted to comfort him in the best way a woman could comfort a man, with her warmth and giving of herself. He'd been too desperately hungry for her to analyze her motives that night. But when he found out she'd filed for divorce the next day, he realized the truth about that night. At first he had reacted with anger. But now he was facing reality. It was not easy to keep his hands off Natalie. He longed for her with every fiber of his being. But he had no right to her until he could resolve his own failure.

There would be no problem if they completed the production. He was as certain of its success as he was of tomorrow's sunrise. The hitch lay in whether or not they could complete it. He had to face the fact that if he was going to turn out the motion picture he visualized it was going to take more time and money than the original budget—a lot more time and a lot more money.

He was drawn out of his reverie by Marsha's voice. "I can see why you love her so," Marsha said wistfully. "Natalie is as cool and exquisite as a very expensive, frosty bottle of champagne. She has so much poise, such class. So much beauty. And yet, in spite of all the money in her family and her own success, she's not the slightest bit stuck-up. She treats the lowest grip on the set with consideration, just like her own equal."

Kirk nodded, again sinking into his own thoughts. He thought of the difference in their backgrounds. Natalie's wealthy family setting, Swiss finishing school, and his own middle-class family where keeping up the house rent and the payments on a second-hand car was the big deal. They came from different worlds. Only if he achieved his goals would he have lifted himself by his bootstraps to her level.

Aloud, he said, "I've got to pull off this film and get back on my feet before I have a right to be Natalie's husband. I have to show her that I wasn't just using her to get the studio to back the film. . . ."

"And what if it fails?"

"Then, I guess it's back to Europe and obscurity for me. This time for keeps."

Marsha shook her head slowly. "Male ego! If Natalie really loves you and if she's worth anything at all, she wouldn't care if you're a big success or not."

"Yeah, but I'd care. It would eat at me and destroy everything between us. I'd be living off her income, a kept man. I'd hate her and we'd wind up hating each other."

She reached for his hand, her huge, dark eyes gazing directly into his. In a husky voice she said, "Kirk, it wouldn't make any difference to me if you never made another motion picture. I'd take you on any terms. And you can have me on any terms." Color rose to her cheeks as she said in a low voice, "In fact, you can have me tonight, if you want—no strings, no demands. . . ."

Kirk felt the warmth of her hand. He squeezed his fingers. "That's very tempting, Marsha. You're a beautiful woman and I value you highly as a friend. But right now—"

She sighed, withdrawing her hand. "I know. You're too hung up on Natalie to get involved with another woman, especially with Natalie in the same hotel. I can understand that. Just remember, honey, I'm not one to give up easily. I'm going to keep right on trying, every chance I get, so Natalie had better watch out."

He smiled. "Is that a threat?"

She shrugged. "All's fair . . ."

Kirk saw Marsha back to the hotel and then he walked along the beach for a while, thinking about his personal and professional problems. He wondered what life's ironies and contradictions had in store for him. Would the studio give him the necessary financial support to complete this film? Would he prove himself and win Natalie back? Or would the production end in disaster, leaving his life in shambles?

Would Natalie go through with the divorce or would she change her mind? Would this film make his reputation as the most brilliant, promising young director in Hollywood, or would he go down in defeat? Would he end up back in Europe, perhaps with Marsha Sanders at his side as Natalie faded into a memory along with his film-making dreams?

He felt a chill as he plodded along the beach. His future was one big, ominous question mark.

Chapter Nine

𝒯he next morning, Natalie had breakfast at a table that gave her a firsthand view of Copacabana Beach.

The hotel where she and most of the cast were staying was located on the wide seafront thoroughfare, the Avenida Atlantica. It was an area of waterfront bars bright with neon signs, pavement mosaics and terraced restaurants. Stretched before them, glistening white, was Copacabana Beach. To the west, the Avenida Atlantica curved into the Avenida Vieira Souto and Avenida Delfim Moreira and the beach became Ipanema.

She ate slowly, savoring the sweet, succulent taste of Brazilian fruits, guava, fruta-de-conde and pawpaw and the juice of the maracuja. As she sipped a cup of strong, black Brazilian coffee, she gazed out at the scene on the beach which was already becoming crowded with sun-worshipers.

"Hi, you're up early."

The masculine voice interrupting her thoughts startled her. She swung around to look into the eyes of Tom Sacks. The leading man was as macho handsome as usual. He was dressed for the beach, wearing trunks and a beach robe. "Mind if I join you?"

"Not at all," Natalie said, nodding to the chair across from her.

Sacks slid into the chair. He nodded at Natalie's attire, which also consisted of a swimsuit and robe. "Guess we're planning the same kind of morning."

"Yes, I've been dying to get to the beach."

"Yeah, we might as well relax while we can," Sacks said. "Once we start shooting those Carnival scenes, Kirk is going to run us all ragged."

Natalie gave him a questioning glance. She wondered how far they were going to get into the movie before Kirk and Tom came to blows.

"You don't like him much, do you?"

Sacks shrugged. "I think the feeling is mutual. I know he wanted somebody else for my part. He doesn't think I can act."

Natalie shrugged. "I think you're doing a fine job so far."

Sacks gave a short, angry laugh. "I doubt if Kirk shares that opinion." Then he said to the waitress who appeared at the table, "Just a cup of coffee, please." Addressing Natalie again, he said, "I notice he isn't sparing your feelings, either."

Natalie thought about the humiliating episode on the set when Kirk said her interpretation of Rebecca Abrahms was all wrong. She flushed, feeling a fresh wave of anger.

There was a moment of silence as Sacks stared moodily out at the beach. Suddenly he caught Natalie completely by surprise by saying, "In spite of all that, as much as it galls me, I have to admit he's a helluva good director. There are times when I hate his guts. I want to swing a punch at him. But at the same time, I have to admire his ability. He knows exactly what he wants and, as mad as it makes me, I have to admit he's right. I have been getting by on personality and looks in most of the things I've done lately. The part in this film calls for a lot more. Before it's over, I'm going to find out if I actually can act." Then Sacks grinned. "Did he really throw Sam Kasserman off the barge in the Hudson River that time?"

Natalie shrugged. "He's never talked to me about it, but knowing Kirk, the story is probably true."

"From what I've seen of Kirk Trammer, it's true all right," Sacks continued, nodding. "When he starts a project, it's his production and too bad for anyone who tries to interfere. It's going to get him in trouble this time, though," Sacks muttered.

Natalie raised an eyebrow. "Is that a threat?"

"Just an observation. I'm thinking about the home office. D'you know we've hardly gotten started and already he's behind shooting schedule and over budget?"

"Yes," Natalie said uncomfortably.

"Wait until this thing really starts rolling, all that outer space special effects stuff, the scenes he's planning to shoot in the desert in Tunisia. Natalie, the cost is going to go through the roof. I can see disaster looming. I can hear the studio howling already."

Sacks finished his coffee. "Well, that's his problem, isn't it?"

"Yes," Natalie replied absently. To herself, she thought that wasn't exactly true. It wasn't only Kirk's problem. She was still too angry thinking about Kirk and Marsha together last night to give a hang what became of him. But she was concerned for the sake of the movie and her friends who were involved, to say nothing of her own career.

"Well," Tom Sacks said, unwinding his large frame from the chair, "the beach beckons. Shall we go soak up some of this fine Brazilian sunshine?"

"All right."

On the beach, they set up a miniature encampment consisting of umbrellas, beach mats and portable radios.

The brilliant February midsummer sun was blinding on the white sand, making sunglasses mandatory. From the tropical jungles in the mountains overlooking the city came butterflies in bright rainbow colors, fluttering down over the beach and surf.

By now the beach was teeming with life, crowded with sun-bronzed bodies. There were joggers thudding by in strides that kicked up little spurts of sand, groups of young people playing football, and others working out on a gymnastic apparatus. There was a constant parade of young women like healthy amazons, their perfectly sculpted bodies scantily clad in string bikinis, strolling past older citizens who sat patiently absorbing the ultraviolet rays.

Threading their way in the crowd in dogged, perpetual motion, were the beach vendors laden with stacks of bright red, yellow, green and blue hats; balancing baskets of pineapples on their heads; staggering along with heavy containers of cold lemonade, soft drinks or beer, all crying out their sales pitch above the sound of the surf and the portable radios.

Natalie sensed an undercurrent of tension, a kind of expectant excitement in the air. She had felt it everywhere she went in the city. It was anticipation of the Carnival soon to begin. There was a feeling that the whole city was holding its breath, counting off the minutes until it would explode in a shattering frenzy of revelry.

"Have you ever been here at Carnival time?" Natalie asked.

Tom nodded. "A couple of years ago. It's mass hysteria from Sunday through Tuesday night, right up to Ash Wednesday. The entire city goes mad. Everyone sheds conventional restraints in one big continuous party." He chuckled. "On Ash Wednesday morning, the entire city wakes up with a colossal hangover."

Natalie smiled. "Sounds like fun."

"Oh, it is. Especially if you're with the right person." He gave her a long, thoughtful look as he said the words.

Natalie suddenly felt a wave of self-consciousness. Tom's gaze trailed over her curves generously revealed by the skimpy bikini. She was acutely conscious of the male approval and interest in what he saw.

Her cheeks flushing, she stammered, "I doubt if anyone in the cast is going to have much time for partying. Kirk has a heavy shooting schedule planned. He wants to use the Carnival activity in several scenes."

"Yeah, I know," Tom muttered. "Still, we might be able to sneak off for a little Carnival fun. How about it, Natalie?"

"I'm not promising anything," she parried.

A smile touched a corner of his lips as he continued to study her in a contemplative manner. "How are things with you and Kirk?"

She frowned. "What do you mean?"

"I mean on a personal level."

"Then that's personal, isn't it?"

He shrugged. "Stars don't have much privacy, as you know. It's common knowledge that you've filed for divorce."

The conversation was taking a direction that made her uncomfortable. Impulsively, she jumped up, dusting grains of sand from her hips. "Come on, we're wasting that beautiful water. Last one in is a monkey's uncle!"

Tom laughed, uncoiling his six-foot frame and rising to his feet. They raced to the water's edge and plunged into the foaming surf. At first the breakers knocked Natalie off balance, sending her sprawling on the sandy bottom, from which she came up spluttering salt water. But then she battled her way past the crashing breakers to the gentle swells where she swam easily and floated for a while, rocked in rhythmic, soothing motion by the sea. Out here it was warm and peaceful after the noise and confusion of the beach.

As she looked back at the city she had the sensation of the buildings and skyscrapers swaying back and forth before her eyes. She thought it was a city forever trapped between the sea in front of it and the jungle-covered mountains behind it. Above it all, the huge statue of Christ gazed solemnly down from the mountain top, arms outstretched in permanent benediction.

The great distance of the ocean horizon on the one side and the mountains dissolving in clouds and mists on the other gave it all the illusion of a dream city floating in space.

Tom challenged her to a race. He was a powerful swimmer. The corded muscles of his shoulders and arms swelled and rippled as he plowed through the water.

Natalie, a good swimmer herself, managed to keep up with him for a while, but then surrendered and came to a breathless stop, glad to find the sandy bottom under her feet.

Tom turned to join her, breathing hard, too.

For a few moments they were too busy catching their breath to speak. Then they both burst out laughing. Natalie felt carefree and gay in the sparkling water, enjoying one of those fleeting moments when time evaporated and she was a child again.

Suddenly, Tom bent forward and his lips brushed hers. She was startled, frozen by shock. Ever since he'd joined her for breakfast, Natalie had been aware of his interest in her. She had been struggling with this development, not sure how to deal with it. Kirk had been the only man in her life. Even during their estrangement, when he was in Europe, she had avoided entanglements, becoming something of a recluse except for her closest friends. But now, making this movie, she was thrown together with one of

the world's most eligible and attractive male stars.
Women would cut their wrists for a chance to be with
Tom Sacks.

"How about us, Natalie?" Tom asked, gazing directly into her eyes. His arms were around her lightly
as the motion of the waves swayed their bodies,
making them touch. "You're a gorgeous woman. I'm
between wives. You're divorcing Kirk. Fate has
thrown us together. Don't you think we should do
something about it?"

It was a challenge that gave her a strange feeling.
How did she feel about Tom Sacks—or any other
man for that matter? She couldn't answer that
question. Until now, her life and emotions had been
too entangled with Kirk. This situation made her
understand clearly why she had to divorce Kirk; it
was the only way she could get on with her own
life.

"Tom . . . give me a little time, okay?"

He shrugged. "We'd be a great pair, Natalie. Think
about it."

Then he turned and swam back to the beach.

Natalie followed at a slower pace, her thoughts
chaotic. Under their umbrella they sipped cooling
drinks Tom bought from a beach vendor, and made
small talk. After a while, made drowsy by the swim
and warm sunlight, Natalie rolled over on her stomach, resting her cheek on the back of one hand.
Vaguely, she heard Tom say something about going
back to the hotel for a while.

She dozed off.

She was awakened by the touch of a hand on her
shoulder. She raised her head sleepily, thinking Tom

had returned, and she looked directly into a pair of hazel eyes.

Natalie jerked upright with a gasp. Kirk's face was inches away.

He put some more suntan lotion in the palm of his hand and continued to smooth it into her shoulder. He said, "You're going to get a heck of a burn. Don't you know you can't lie out here in the summer sun without some protection?"

"What are you doing here?" she demanded.

"Well, at the moment, I'm trying to keep you from turning red as a lobster."

"How did you know I was out here?"

"I didn't come looking for you if that's what you mean. I was strolling along the beach and saw you coming out of the water like a sea nymph. A lovely sea nymph, I might add." His teeth flashed white in a lean grin.

She jerked away from him. "I don't need your ministrations. If I want to get a sunburn that's my business."

"Not entirely. You can get sick from too much sun and cost us several days of shooting."

"That's all you care about, isn't it, Kirk Trammer?" she fumed. "I could die of sunstroke and you wouldn't give a hang so long as it didn't interfere with your precious shooting schedule."

"My, aren't we in a friendly mood this morning."

"Whatever makes you think we're friends?"

His hazel eyes gave her a long, contemplative look. "Why should we be enemies?"

"Plenty of reasons. I don't think I need to list them."

He continued to gaze directly into her eyes with a strange, dark expression that was disconcerting. "Are you sure?"

"Absolutely." Then, she nervously changed the subject. "Kirk, it was absolutely rotten of you to chew me out in front of the entire set over the way I'm handling my role. I'm furious with you for doing that."

"Sorry. I didn't mean to humiliate you. But it's for your own good, Natalie."

"I don't need you telling me what's for my own good. I think you're dead wrong about the way I'm handling the part of Rebecca Abrahms. In spite of her background, the woman has class. You want me to rob her of that."

"No. I want you to make her more believable."

"That's only your opinion. I know my job, Kirk."

"I didn't say you don't. Anyway, this argument is getting us nowhere. Why don't you shut up and let me put some of this lotion on your back before you turn into a lobster?"

"Go put it on Marsha Sanders's back!"

"Oh, now I'm getting the real picture of why you're so mad. It really isn't the argument about the role in the movie. It's Marsha. You're jealous."

"Don't be ridiculous. But you could be a little more discreet. If you must bring your mistress along, you don't have to humiliate me by carrying on with her in front of the whole cast."

"Who says she's my mistress?"

"Don't make me out to be a fool, Kirk. It's obvious to the whole world."

"Well, it was pretty obvious to the world what you

and Tom Sacks are up to," he said grimly. "I saw you kissing him out in the water."

"Then you were spying on me!" She gasped.

"No. I told you, I was walking along the beach. I just happened to see you. It doesn't matter. You're free to do what you want. Only don't go making cracks about Marsha and me when you're having a fling with Tom Sacks."

"I'm not having a 'fling' with anybody. Tom and I are just friends. That kiss meant nothing."

Why was she defending herself, she asked herself furiously. She didn't have to explain her actions to Kirk.

Anyway, she doubted that he believed her.

His palm, feeling warm and moist, moved in a steady, rotating motion over her shoulders and neck.

She closed her eyes, fighting the tingling warmth of nerve ends under his touch. His broad, strong hand moved lower, to her shoulder blades. An involuntary shudder ran through her body. Her voice was slightly thick as she muttered, "That's enough. You can stop now."

"No, you're still exposing a lot of bare skin to the sun. You need more of this sunblock. Stretch out on your tummy and relax."

She hated herself for meekly obeying but the will to resist was melting as if being drained by the soothing touch of his moving hand. She turned onto her stomach, nestling her face against the back of her hand, rationalizing that she could suffer a dangerous sunburn if her skin were unprotected.

She murmured an objection when he unfastened the strap of her halter top, but her voice seemed weak and faraway. With her back uncovered, he smoothed the lotion from her neck down to the base of her spine. His hands were confident, exploring familiar territory. The thought of how well those hands knew her body made her face grow hot. Her body became limp under the massaging application of the lotion.

Why was she allowing him to do this? He wasn't just applying a coat of sunblock. He was turning his task into a seductive massage that was making her drowsy and vulnerable. She became dreamily conscious of the sights and sounds around her as if they reached her senses through a soft haze.

She felt the grains of sand, gently gritty under her stomach and thighs. Above them a sea bird swooped and called. The sound of children's voices raised in a game of tag mingled with the swish of the surf. A beach vendor trudging by was calling his sales pitch, crying, in Portuguese, *"Alo, alo. Tomando limonada,"* assuring all the women on the beach that if they drank his lemonade they would become beautiful. A radio under a nearby beach umbrella was playing a familiar song of Rio, *Garota de Ipanema*— "Girl from Ipanema."

Mostly she was aware of Kirk's presence, his nearness. He was kneeling beside her, his strong leg inches from her face. Opening her eyes, she could see the curling brown hair on his bare thigh, the masculine texture of his skin. She bit her lip, struggling to quiet the waves of desire that stirred deep within her, beginning to radiate through her entire body. She was furious with herself. How could she still experience the reawakening of old passions, knowing how utterly selfish Kirk was? Why did she have to remind herself over and over that his only interest in her was using her to get studio backing for this picture?

His palm, hard yet gentle, rippled over her back, sometimes in circles, sometimes moving slowly up and down her spine. The warmth of the sun, the rhythm of the surf, the caressing massage of Kirk's hand conspired to put her in a trance.

Unbidden memories were creeping into her thoughts, scenes of the past with Kirk, a time in Mexico, a hotel room in Acapulco, sea breezes stirring the curtains at an open window, Kirk giving her a massage, starting with her back until waves of heat were coursing through her body and she turned over, raising her arms and his lips crushed hers and their bodies became one, closer . . . closer . . . closer. . . .

It was a daydream that made her stretch languorously like a kitten, warm and lazy in the sun. Then the sound of Kirk's voice brought her back to the present.

"A strange and beautiful city," Kirk murmured, gazing around as he applied the suntan lotion. "I was reading up on its history. Captain Goncalvés entered Guanabara Bay on the first of January in 1502. He thought he'd found a great river and that's how the city got its name, Rio de Janeiro, the River of January."

His gaze lifted to the towering mountains behind and above the city, dark green with tangled jungle growth. The hazel color of his eyes became more intense. "Back there, in the mountains—that's where we're going to shoot the Central American revolutionary scenes. The setting is perfect. The topography is the same as Central America. All South American jungles look alike to a movie audience."

Natalie's drowsy, half-somnolent state dissolved. She frowned, coming totally awake with a start. "What are you talking about?"

"I was up there late yesterday. It's only an hour away by 'copter. I've signed the lease for the location. Mountains, jungle trails, a waterfall. It's fabulous."

Natalie sat up, clutching her halter top. "Are you out of your mind? There's nothing in the script about any jungle scene. After the Carnival we're scheduled to fly to Tunisia."

"I just changed the schedule. This is too good to pass up. I don't know how we could have overlooked something like this when we were working on the script. It's obvious, isn't it, that this kind of international intrigue would include the conflict going on in Central America? It would be totally logical for the heroine in the story to go from Rio to Central America. We can develop some great action stuff—jeep chase scenes through the brush, a guerrilla shoot-out in a village, the hero and heroine being shot at in the jungle, escaping over the waterfall. . . ."

Natalie felt a sinking sensation in the pit of her stomach. "Jeeps—villages . . . Kirk, where are you going to get those kinds of props?"

"The lease area includes a deserted village. We can fly some jeeps up there by helicopter."

"But you're talking about taking a whole army of extras up there! To say nothing of the guns, the explosives—"

"Right. We'll need to take Ginny Wells temporarily

off the space sets she's building in Los Angeles and fly her down here to handle the effects. We're going to need some stunt people, too. I don't think you're going to want to go over a cliff and into a waterfall. I know Tom Sacks doesn't want to. Might mess up his gorgeous profile." He chuckled dryly.

Natalie was staring at him, wide-eyed. She felt a torrent of emotions churning inside her and was dismayed at the cost this extra shooting was going to involve. Yet it was impossible to ignore the excitement Kirk could generate. It was as if his surge of enthusiasm set off electric shock waves in the air that radiated into her being, shooting sparks through her nerve ends.

She felt herself tremble both from apprehension and excitement. "Kirk, the studio won't stand for the extra expense. You're going to blow the budget before you're halfway through the film. This is exactly the kind of thing Sam Kasserman was afraid of."

"Hang Sam Kasserman," Kirk muttered. "He's not making this film."

"It's the studio's money, and he's responsible."

Kirk dismissed that with an impatient hand gesture. "He'll get it back many times over. This motion picture is going to be the biggest money-maker of the year."

Natalie shook her head, at a loss to know what to say. She knew when Kirk made up his mind about something like this nothing would change it.

Then Kirk said, "First we have to deal with the Carnival sequence and the scenes aboard the yacht. I want you to have dinner with me on the yacht tonight."

She was instantly on guard. "Why?"

"I want you to meet the owner, for one thing. He's a big fan of yours. You know the type. Corporation president. All titillated by the chance to meet Hollywood stars firsthand. That's why he's practically giving us the yacht to use."

"I see," Natalie retorted angrily. "I'm being useful again for you to get what you want."

"Don't get on your high horse. You'll enjoy it. Great dinner. He's got a French chef on board. Beautiful view. Give you a chance to familiarize yourself with the setting."

"All right," she said coldly. "As long as it's strictly business. That's the only kind of dealings I want to have with you, Kirk Trammer!"

Angrily she reached back and fastened her halter. She jumped up and ran into the surf to get away from him. She swam furiously and after a while, looked back. Kirk was gone.

Chapter Ten

From the eighty-foot luxury yacht, *Allegretto,* gently swaying in the harbor, the view was breathtaking. Across the bay, the lights of the city twinkled like a great ring of diamonds. High in the background at the 2,307-foot peak of Mount Corcovado, the great statue of Christ illuminated by floodlights had been reduced to a miniature at a distance. A mist had settled over the mountaintops creating an unearthly translucent glow around the statue, giving the eerie impression that it floated in space.

The evening was warm and sultry. Natalie had dressed appropriately in a filmy evening formal that left her shoulders bare. When Kirk picked her up at the hotel, he had surprised her by appearing in a white dinner jacket.

"Where did you get that dinner jacket?" she asked.

"What's the matter? Doesn't it fit?"

"It fits fine. It's just that I so rarely see you in anything but faded jeans, boots and that old rumpled jacket of yours that the transformation into formal wear is something of a shock."

"Well, I rented it if you must know. I thought the occasion called for something more formal. It isn't every night we get to have dinner on a millionaire's yacht."

Natalie tried to limit her gaze, but it was hard not to look at him. Living on the beach at Malibu had given him a golden tan that had been refreshed by the midsummer sun here in Rio. It created a dashing, handsome contrast to the white jacket. The deep tan made his hazel eyes appear to be a lighter golden brown. Only his bushy hair was the same as usual, rebelliously defying any attempt at being combed.

Uneasily, she looked away and maintained a cool silence on the way to the docks. There they were met by the yacht's crew members, helped into a tender and swept out to the anchored yacht where they were greeted by another crew member, escorted to deck chairs and served cocktails.

Natalie had the sensation of being on a romantic movie set. She was surrounded by the luxurious gleam of polished brass and the soft patina of rich mahogany and teak. A gentle sea breeze wafted across the deck, caressing her cheeks and teasing a strand of her hair. She thought that the owner of such a beautiful craft had to be enormously wealthy.

"When do I meet the owner?" Natalie asked.

Kirk sipped his highball. "I forgot to tell you. He phoned late this afternoon. Had to grab a flight back to New York. Some kind of corporate crisis. But he insisted that we come on out anyway since he already had the dinner planned.''

Her eyes narrowed. A protest was rising to her lips, but they were interrupted by a waiter beginning to serve their meal.

From the sterling silver to fine china and crystal, the standard of luxury and exquisite taste was maintained. Kirk hadn't exaggerated about the French chef. The meal began with sherry, *consommé à la royale* and *pâté maison*. There was a flaming entrée, crêpes and vintage champagne.

Romantic dinner music floated on the evening air from deck speakers. Natalie ate slowly, savoring the rich exquisite flavors, the delicious champagne.

After the meal, Kirk took her on a tour of the vessel. There was a piano in a lounge where he took a seat, his fingers rippling an arpeggio over the keys, then settling into the rich chords of a romantic ballad. Natalie settled into a plush chair, sipping her champagne, closing her eyes as the melody Kirk was playing reached tender spots in her emotions. For reasons she couldn't define, she felt close to tears.

Kirk played for a while, then they strolled out on deck again and leaned on the rail, gazing across the water at the romantic city of Rio. She was acutely conscious of Kirk's broad shoulder touching hers. A warning voice inside told her she shouldn't be here, but it was faint and too easily ignored.

She was aware of Kirk's gaze. She suddenly felt the need to take a deep breath. Kirk's strong, tanned hand reached for hers. Gently, he turned her to face him.

"Kirk, don't start this," she said, swallowing hard.

"Why not?"

"Because it's only going to wind up making us both miserable. It's over between us, Kirk. I told you I was going to do this picture with you, but it would be strictly business."

He touched her chin, lifting her face so she had to meet his steady gaze. "Are you sure you want to keep it strictly business?"

He had pulled her closer so their bodies were touching. She felt his warmth through the thin fabric of her gown. When she breathed, her breasts were against his chest. She felt the touch of their thighs, the brush of her waist against his. "Yes . . . strictly business . . ." she said weakly.

"I don't believe you."

"All right," she whispered angrily. "You get me out here in this romantic setting . . . the food, the wine . . . the music. . . . How do you expect me to react?"

A half smile tugged at his lips. "Just the way you're reacting now. Natalie, we've made love too often for me not to know your moods. Right now you want me just the way I want you."

Tears blurred her vision. "I should never have come out here with you tonight. You tricked me. Kirk, you're always doing that to me. You're smarter than I am. I'm such a darn patsy! I bet you knew on the beach this morning that your millionaire buddy wasn't going to be here tonight. I bet you cooked this whole scene up with him."

Kirk shook his head, looking innocent, but she didn't believe him.

He bent and his lips brushed hers, bringing a whimper from her throat. His lips touched hers again and again, growing bolder each time. He pulled her closer. The warmth of his body against hers became a flaming torch.

His palms were mashed against her back, molding her body to his. The crew member had cleared away the dinner dishes and discreetly disappeared somewhere below. They were completely alone here.

Kirk's kisses trailed from her lips to her bare shoulders. She began trembling. Then Kirk scooped her up and carried her to a secluded lounge under a canopy on the deck. He nestled there with her, cuddling her, kissing and caressing her. Natalie was breathing hard, consumed by an awakened desire that had become overpowering. Too well her body remembered the passion she had shared with Kirk in the past. The memory of sensation piled on sensation, of fiery caresses and engulfing fulfillment, turned her into a limp victim.

With practiced fingers that had traveled this course many times before, he pulled down the zipper of her dress and unfastened her bra. She gasped as his lips found the hollow between her breasts and his cheek, rough with a faint masculine stubble, brushed the tender creamy skin.

Again following a familiar path, his hands moved down her body, tracing a fiery path over every curve of her waist and hips, down to the hem of her dress, which he brushed up out of the way. His caresses sought the yielding flesh of her thighs. She gasped and dug her fingers into his luxurious hair. She had always loved the feel of its thick, unruly tangle. Her cheek was pressed to his now as he took command of her body.

There was a silence disturbed only by their breathing.

"You like that, don't you?" he whispered.

"Ummm."

"And that . . ."

"Kirk, don't. You're driving me out of my mind."

"That's the idea. Remember that time we were out in the desert in the dune buggies and the sun went down and we wrapped up in blankets and made love on the ground under the stars."

Warm tears filled her eyes. "I wish you wouldn't keep bringing up the past, Kirk. That's all over. . . ." But her voice lacked conviction. She closed her eyes as the gentle swaying of the ship formed a rhythm with the universe. It carried her dangerously close to a sea of passion where the waves rocked back and forth and then leaped into a crashing burst of foaming breakers.

Oh, Kirk, what kind of hold do you have over me? she thought desperately. *Is it possible that I do still love you in spite of everything?*

Why else would she have accepted the role in this film, knowing Kirk was only using her to get the studio financing? Was it only because she felt sorry for him—felt some kind of obligation because of their marriage vows? Questions . . . questions . . . that she could not answer.

She was a first-class fool if she did still love him. Kirk gave her nothing in return except heartache and humiliation. Knowing that, how could she succumb so foolishly to his charms? Logic could not explain the way his touch could bring goosebumps to her flesh, the way her heart would suddenly pound when she caught sight of his broad shoulders, the way his golden tan eyes could reach to the very depths of her being.

Was it only physical attraction? The overwhelming chemistry that could draw a man and woman together was a mystery as old as the human race. It had driven men and women to desperate lengths, had toppled kingdoms, raised hopes to the stars and dashed them to the depths.

Now it threatened her with fresh disaster. Giving in to the desire Kirk had awakened in her would bless her with a few intense, insane moments of paradise, then crush her to fresh agony.

If she hoped to continue with this film production, she simply had to keep herself from falling into the old trap of Kirk's charm. She had to maintain a professional, impersonal relationship with him.

Summoning a strength she didn't know she had, she drew away from him. "No, Kirk," she said firmly. "I am not going to let you make love to me. It won't solve a thing between us. I'm having a hard enough time as it is dealing with this whole situation. I never wanted to do this film with you in the first place. Somehow I let everybody, including you, talk me into it. It's making a nervous wreck out of me. Stirring up old feelings like this isn't helping at all."

His gaze burned into her, making her quiver to the depths of her being. She knew with a mingled feeling of despair and longing that if he persisted, he could still break down the last shred of her resistance.

His eyes burned with such intensity it made her head swim. She wondered if she were going to faint.

Then, after an unbearably tense moment that lasted

an eternity, he settled back against the cushions of the deck lounge. He lit a cigarette and gazed moodily across the bay at the lights of Rio.

The respite gave Natalie a chance to assemble the wreckage of her emotions while she covered her legs and adjusted her clothing. She inhaled the night sea air, making an attempt to steady her nerves. She forced her vision to concentrate on the peaceful scene of the stars above, the smooth water flecked with spots of phosphorescence, the vision of the romantic city across the bay.

Kirk suddenly broke the silence. "Natalie, there's something important I need to talk to you about. I mentioned it this morning—the Central American scenes I want to add to the film. You will help me convince Kasserman, won't you? He likes you. You're important to the studio. I know you can help me make him see that the extra expense will be well worth it."

Natalie felt as if she had been doused with a pail of cold water. If there had been lingering traces of the golden romantic mood, they now vanished completely. She was blinded with fury. "You lousy rat!" she cried. "So that's what this big romantic buildup is all about. The setting, the food, the wine, the sweet talk. Phony, phony, phony! You've had nothing on your mind all evening except to seduce me into helping you talk the studio into additional financing! Kirk Trammer, I despise you!"

"Now wait a minute!" he exclaimed heatedly. "I did not try to seduce you just to get your help. I resent your implying such a thing. What kind of a heel do you think I am?"

"At the moment, I'm not sure."

"Do you really believe that I could stoop that low?"

She gazed at him with cool appraisal. "Frankly, I wouldn't put it past you. Kirk, you're absolutely ruthless when it comes to motion picture making. You have what amounts to an obsession to complete this film. You'd stop at nothing to do it!"

Their eyes locked in deadly combat. In that moment, they were total strangers.

He had resolved not to touch Natalie again until the film was completed, until he had proven himself both to the world and to her. That fine resolve had gone out the window tonight. Seeing her so desirable, while at the same time he was burning inside with the thought of Tom Sacks possessing her, had made him lose all control.

Kirk was fuming. Why had he brought her out here? More important, why had he tried to make love to her? It was a question that defied an answer. Ever since this morning when he caught sight of Natalie in Tom Sacks's arms, kissing in the surf, he had been operating in an emotional whirlpool. He wanted to rearrange Tom Sacks's matinee idol profile. Jealous? Yes, and what a fool he was to have that reaction!

"You know, you're absolutely right," he said with cold fury. "We should get a divorce!"

Chapter Eleven

During the filming of *The Last Encounter* in Rio, a small brick building on a side street had been rented to house the production company. It was an old building with high ceilings and tiled floors that had once housed government offices. Ceiling fans revolved in an effort to dissipate the summer heat. The offices were constantly bustling with activity, a medley of rattling typewriters, voices, jangling telephones and heels tapping on the tile. Shades had been drawn against the glare of the February summer sun.

One room had been converted into a small, makeshift auditorium where a projector flashed the dailies on a screen.

It was several days after the Mardi Gras Carnival had ended. With some of the principals, Natalie sat in the darkened room, watching the fragmented segments that had been shot during and after the Carnival. Even in these rough, uncut and unedited scraps of film she saw how well Kirk had captured the mood of the city during those colorful days of abandoned frenzy and how it had all been integrated into the mood of intrigue and menace in the story they were filming. He had an instinctive knowledge of how to block a scene and how to use camera angles to emphasize an effect.

One scene introduced the assassin who had been sent to Rio to dispatch Rebecca Abrahms. To stress the feeling of threat, the camera was at street level, to catch the wheels of a car skidding to a stop. Then the camera cut to the heavy boots of a man as he stepped out of the car, before it gradually panned upward, silhouetting the assassin against the sun, throwing his face into dark shadows and giving him the impact of overwhelming strength and power. It was powerful and effective cinematography.

The drama was played against the crowded frenzy of the Carnival weekend. Natalie felt her own emotions churning in tempo to the hysteria.

The *baterias,* the percussion bands, marched down the streets driving the crowds mad with their *samba* beats. The *surdo,* the huge bass drum of the *samba* bands, rocked the earth. Drumsticks bounced, tambourines rattled. Dancers in flashing costumes whirled and gyrated. The surging heartbeat of the *samba* was pounded out on an array of Latin rhythm instruments.

Natalie's head pounded, her senses reeled as the scenes unfolded. Half the time she was Rebecca Abrahms, jostled and crushed by the surging crowds, caught in a life-threatening situation. Half the time she was Natalie Brooks, embroiled in her own personal turmoil that was tearing her apart.

Why couldn't Kirk have stayed in Europe! Then she would have been spared this ongoing torment that matched the anguish of the woman she was playing on the screen.

She tried to concentrate on the action in the film.

Rio had been preparing for months for these few days of uninhibited revelry leading up to Ash Wednesday. Since May of the year before, the *samba* schools had chosen the theme they would carry out in the parades. By government decree, the theme of the costumes, floats and dances must portray some part of Brazilian history or culture.

By August musicians had composed new *sambas* that would fit the chosen theme. Artists and designers got busy creating the *fantasias*—the extravagant, glittering costumes and the enormous floats called *alegorios*. By November, the *samba* dancers had settled down to hard, grinding rehearsals, preparing for the day they would parade through the streets of Rio.

During the week leading up to the Carnival, workmen had been constructing grandstands along the Avenida Presidente Vargas and Avenida Rio Braca, the main section of downtown Rio where the *desfiles*, the public parades, would pass.

There, Natalie saw herself being jostled by throngs of revelers in outlandish and grotesque costumes. Red-faced Satans leered at her. Skeletons leaped around. Men were dressed as women with grotesque painted lips and exaggerated bosoms. There were clowns, slave girls, Frankenstein monster masks, werewolves and bunny rabbits.

There was a "clack" as another blackboard marker with the scene and take numbers scribbled on it appeared on the screen.

Then, out of the crowd emerged a man, touching her arm. "Rebecca Abrahms? Come with me."

A quick zooming closeup of her pale, stricken face, eyes wide with terror.

The heat of the day, over a hundred degrees, registered on the perspiring faces and the glaring sun on the pavement. It seemed to radiate from the screen. *Samba* dancers fainted, overcome by the heat. Camera crews had sweated. Rebecca, in the crush of the crowd, had felt her head swimming, had been gripped at times with the panic of claustrophobia. Her clothes, soaked with perspiration, had stuck to her body. Strands of her disheveled hair were glued to her forehead.

"Good," Kirk had exclaimed. "That's the kind of realism I want at this point"—and had chased away the makeup people who wanted to rush in between takes and make repairs to Natalie's face.

She thought grimly that this was certainly going to be a radical departure from the sophisticated, urban roles she had been playing.

In addition to the street scenes, there were some night takes in the setting of abandoned merrymaking that took place at parties and nightclubs.

Finally, there was the effective chase scene that had been filmed at dawn on Wednesday, hours after the frenetic activity of the Carnival had died. An eerie hush had settled over the city. The empty streets were littered with the refuse of revelry: streamers, hats, empty bottles, paper, deserted grandstands, confetti, a wrecked float.

The party was over and everyone had gone home. The camera had panned over the deserted streets. There was an eerie silence. The only movement was a sea bird circling over the quiet beach. There was a close up of a reveler sprawled on the beach, clutching an empty wine bottle, snoring softly, his mouth open, a fly walking unnoticed across his lip.

Then there was a shot of a street. Suddenly, violent action burst upon the screen—an automobile that seemed to leap out of nowhere, directly at the camera. Natalie could imagine the sound effects that would be dubbed in, the whine of tortured motors, the screech of burning rubber as the two cars, one pursuing the other, streaked through the streets.

Various camera placements had been used to give the impact of rushing speed. A camera had been mounted behind a driver in one of the vehicles so a fragment of the chase was seen through the windshield of the pursuing car. In another shot, a camera had been mounted just behind the front wheel, so the screen gave the audience a view of the chase from a low angle dominated by the spinning wheel. Other angles were shot from a helicopter to give the broad overhead view of the two racing cars.

Kirk had had two of Hollywood's best stunt-car drivers flown in to do the scene.

Later, back in sound stages prepared by Ginny Wells in Hollywood, there would be shots made of Natalie playing a frightened Rebecca Abrahms in a back seat of a car filmed against a rear projection screen which showed the pursuing car. That would be edited so skillfully into other segments of the chase scene that the audience would believe it was all shot in one take in the streets of Rio.

That afternoon, Natalie went to the airport to meet Ginny Wells, who was flying in from Hollywood.

In the taxi, on their way to the hotel, Ginny had to know how the filming was progressing. "What kind of insanity is Kirk involved in now? I'm up to my ears in those sets for the space scenes and I get this urgent telephone call, 'Drop everything and take the earliest plane to Rio.'"

"Insanity is the right word for it," Natalie agreed. "Kirk has decided to add some jungle scenes depicting Central American involvement in the story."

"Jungle scenes?" Ginny gasped. "Where is he going to get a jungle?"

"Right here in Brazil. He's leased a place somewhere. Don't ask me how. All I know is that the only way in and out is by helicopter."

"He's going to fly camera crews in by helicopter?" Ginny asked, her face registering disbelief.

"Camera crews, jeeps and no telling how many extras. Do you like to work with dynamite?"

"Not particularly, though of course I can do it."

"Well, you might as well get ready to set up some battle scenes. Machine guns, mortars, explosions, jeep chases through the brush . . ."

"Wait a minute. I've read this script a dozen times. How does he plan to fit all that into the story?"

"You recall that in the story Rebecca Abrahms has

stumbled on the plot to destroy the American surveillance space station which keeps other countries from using nuclear warheads. Kirk wants to have her leave Rio and fly to Central America to follow this lead. I suppose it could be worked out to have a Central American military leader in cahoots with the dictator of a small Middle-Eastern country. They're out to destroy the space station and then blackmail the rest of the world with their nuclear device."

Ginny shook her head. "That's going to take a major rewrite. Do Bill and Sally Dentmen know about this?"

"No. So far Kirk has only told me about it. He's calling a meeting of production heads tonight to spring his brilliant idea. That's why he wanted you here today, to give your expertise on the special effects that will be needed."

"Wow. The stuff is going to hit the fan when the studio hears about this! Kirk is already behind shooting schedule. Not to mention the fact that the elaborate sets he wants for the space station scenes are going to cost a lot more than the first studio estimates. To throw in the kind of jungle warfare stuff you're describing can add millions to the budget. They'll never stand for it."

"I know. I tried to tell Kirk that. But you know Kirk Trammer when he's in the throes of creativity." Natalie looked glumly out of the taxi window.

"How do the dailies look so far?"

"Very good," Natalie admitted. "Personal feelings aside, I have to give Kirk credit for being a genius. He's actually got Tom Sacks doing some acting for a change instead of just getting by on his profile and personality. And he's giving me a challenge to do something different. From a professional standpoint it's exciting. Kirk has a sense of pace and timing that's thrilling. He's used camera devices like an artist with a paintbrush or a musician with inventive harmonies to create striking effects—well, you'll have to see some of the rushes to judge for yourself."

"Sounds as if you're excited about the film."

"If it were anyone but Kirk, that could be true."

"You do look tired, though, Natalie."

"I am tired. The shooting schedule has been murder. Kirk won't let up a minute. He's a slave driver. And this awful midsummer heat doesn't help any. Can you believe right now they're having a snow storm in New York!"

"I hope you're not going to make yourself sick," Ginny said in a worried tone.

"I have a hunch we're all going to be basket cases by the time this is over."

In the hotel room, as Ginny was unpacking, she asked casually, "Aside from Kirk's being the usual tyrant on a set, how have you two been getting along?"

"It's an emotional strain," Natalie said, kicking off her shoes and curling her legs under her as she sat on Ginny's bed. "I knew it would be." She felt herself suddenly close to tears.

Ginny sat beside her, giving her hand a warm squeeze. "Any chance of you two patching things up?"

"Of course not! Our marriage is over, Ginny, you know that. I'm just suffering from emotional fall-out."

Natalie's cousin sighed. "I feel guilty in a way. I was one of the bunch that twisted your arm into doing this film with Kirk. I guess I kinda hoped it might bring the two of you back together."

Natalie laughed harshly. "Fat chance! Kirk doesn't care anything about me, except to use me every way he can to get to do this film. The other night, he took me out to a friend's yacht, wined and dined me and tried to seduce me only because he thought it would soften me up and get me on his side. Like a dope, I almost fell for it. Where Kirk is concerned, I'm the world's biggest patsy, Ginny."

There was a moment of silence. Ginny's expression was one of concern and sympathy. "I—I guess you still must care for him in spite of everything. . . ."

"I guess so," Natalie said. "Why else did I get involved in this project in the first place? I could have said no. But I just couldn't stand by and see Kirk lose this last big chance. Well, it's strictly business with him from now until we get through shooting this movie and then I hope I never see Kirk Trammer again as long as I live!"

Late that afternoon, Natalie and Ginger had supper at a sidewalk café. They sat in the shade of a large umbrella and ordered a typical Brazilian dish, *feijoada completa*—black beans, rice and meat.

"I see what you mean by the heat," Ginny said, sipping a tall drink filled with tinkling ice. She touched the frosted glass to her damp temple. "Have you spent any time at the beach?"

"So far, I've only had time to get to the beach one morning. I told you Kirk is running us ragged." Then she added grimly, "Wait until he gets us up in the jungle."

"*If* he gets us up in the jungle," Ginny corrected. "Remember, he still has to sell the studio on the extra expense."

"I guess we're going to start the battle over that tonight at the meeting Kirk has called for the principals and production heads."

Kirk paced restlessly, his hazel eyes flashing sparks as he spoke to the group assembled in the production office. "These additional scenes I plan to do, carrying the story to a Central American setting, are going to add an important dimension to the story. It gives us the opportunity for some tight, dramatic action scenes and heightened suspense."

Natalie glanced around the room, taking in expressions ranging from surprise to stunned disbelief on the faces around her. Sally Dentmen looked pale. Bill, his teeth clamped furiously on a pipe stem, was frowning darkly. He removed the pipe and cleared his throat. "Kirk, you're talking about a major rewrite of the entire story. It's more than throwing in some scenes. We have to make big changes in the story that follows."

"I know that," Kirk said calmly. "That's your job, Bill."

"You're asking for a lot. . . ." Bill Dentmen objected.

The associate producer, Howard Ansco, leaped to his feet, his face livid. Ansco was a slender individual with a nervous habit of blinking rapidly when he talked. He brushed a hand across the thin strands of sandy hair and waved his arms in the air. "Kirk, you can't do this!" His voice was several decibels past yelling.

"Sure I can," Kirk replied calmly.

Ansco made an appealing gesture to the group in the room. "He's insane. Max, tell him he can't do this."

As producer and director, Kirk was commanding general of the film production. His production manager could be likened to the chief of staff. The job was held by a tall, bald individual named Max Singler, dubbed "Max the Clax" for some reason no one could remember. Max had been in film production work for twenty-five years. He looked tired and disillusioned.

Max's job covered a staggering amount of intricate details. The script had been broken into basic segments. Everything was planned to the most minute detail to conform to schedules that included transportation, travel time, hotel accommodations, costumes, even the number of meals needed by the entire company. Included in the careful time schedule was an estimate covering how much time was involved in shooting X number of pages of the script. That information, relayed to the studio offices, gave an indication of how well the director was staying within the budget and on shooting schedule.

Now Max Singler said wearily, "Kirk, you can't do this. You know the studio has approved the script we're working with. It's all been figured down to the last foot of film and minute of shooting time. Already you're in hot water with the home office because you're behind schedule. They expect you to make it up, not add a few million dollars to the budget."

"I'm making a major motion picture," Kirk said coldly. "This is going to be the year's big blockbuster. I'm not going to let some myopic, tightfisted studio heads ruin a chance like this. They'll get their investment back ten times over if they'll keep out of my way."

Chapter Twelve

The Jungle . . .

"All right, people," bawled the assistant director. "Action! Cameras!"

A crew member held a blackboard scene marker in front of the cameras.

Rebecca Abrahms came awake with a start. She looked around the small room with its dirt floor and whitewashed adobe walls. The only furnishings in the room were the bed, two wooden chairs and a ramshackle table. On one wall was a faded bullfight poster beside a picture of Fidel Castro. There was a heavy silence except for the patter of raindrops on the thatched roof and broad-leafed tropical plants outside the window.

Standing tensely near the window was Clay Winters, unclothed except for undershorts. He had drawn back so as not to be visible from the outside as he peered around a broken shutter.

Hearing Rebecca stir, he turned quickly. She started to speak, but he put his finger to his lips. He crossed the room and sat on the edge of the bed.

Rebecca was sitting up, holding the sheet over her bosom. "Clay . . . what is it?" she whispered.

"We have to get out of here," Winters said hoarsely. "There's a patrol of government soldiers out there. I saw them moving through the brush past the clearing. They're watching the house."

"Oh, Clay, I thought we were safe here. . . ."

"Somebody tipped them off. Get dressed. Hurry."

Rebecca swung long, shapely bare legs from under the sheet, off the side of the bed.

The camera panned to the window, framed it, then made a fast zoom to the fringe of jungle where a uniformed officer was holding a pair of binoculars trained on the house.

When the camera turned back to Rebecca Abrahms, she was hastily stuffing the tail of her short-sleeved white shirt into a pair of torn jeans. She sat on the edge of the bed and pulled on boots. On the other side of the bed, Clay Winters was also finishing dressing.

They ran to the door, holding hands. "We have to make a dash for it," Clay said tensely. "I have a feeling they're going to level this house with a mortar shell any minute."

Rebecca's face was pale. The cords in her throat were rigid. Her eyes were large with fright. "They'll open fire on us when we leave the house."

Clay nodded. "I hope if we duck out of here and run fast we can take them by surprise. They think we're still asleep. If we're lucky, we can get into the jeep before they have time to take close aim."

Her arms went around him. She pressed her tear-streaked face against his shoulder. "Clay . . . Clay, it's my fault you're here. Why didn't you stay in Rio?"

"You know why. From now on, whatever happens to one of us happens to both of us, Rebecca."

"Oh, Clay, my darling."

They kissed—a long, searing kiss.

Breathlessly, she continued, "Last night . . . together. Clay, it was heaven. If that's all there's to be, we still had more than most people have in a lifetime."

"I know," he nodded gravely, his eyes focused intensely on hers. "I love you, Rebecca."

"And I, you, my dearest."

He drew a breath. "Ready?"

She swallowed hard. "Yes."

He put his hand on the doorknob. "This has to be fast. I'll kick the door open. Bend over so you'll be partly hidden by the jeep. Run like you've never run before."

She nodded.

The door slammed open.

The two burst from the small adobe building.

Almost at once there was an eruption of machine gun fire from the jungle.

Ginny Wells had planted a row of small explosives, called squibs, in the dirt. As Rebecca Abrahms and Clay Winters ran to the jeep, the squibs were touched off by remote wiring. The effect was the very realistic appearance of a hail of machine gun fire kicking up the dirt around their feet as they ran a zigzag course to the waiting jeep.

At the same time, Ginny closed another switch that set off dynamite charges planted in the adobe house. It exploded with an ear-shattering crash, hurling a cloud of shattered adobe clay sky high. On the screen it would look like the result of a direct mortar shell hit.

Clay and Rebecca piled into the jeep.

At that point, Kirk signaled his assistant director, who bawled, "Cut!" through his bullhorn.

The guns in the brush stopped firing their fusillade of blanks. A momentary hush settled with the dust from the squibs and the dynamite explosion.

Natalie wrenched herself out of the character of Rebecca Abrahms and scrambled from the jeep, followed by Tom Sacks. Their places were taken by a stunt man and stunt woman wearing identical clothing and makeup.

"All right," bawled the A.D. through his bullhorn. "Let's get right back with it before the sun changes. Cameras one, two and three. Let's roll 'em. Action. You guys in the trees start shooting. Damn, how do you say 'start shooting' in Portuguese?"

He handed the bullhorn to an interpreter who had been hired to communicate with the extras.

Natalie ran out of the camera range and watched the action sequence.

The jeep starter spun furiously, but the engine didn't catch.

"Cut! What the hell's th' matter with the jeep?"

The stunt man held up his hands in a gesture of helplessness. "Won't start."

Kirk gave vent to his exasperation in a string of expletives. "I knew the guy who sold us those jeeps was a crook. Where are the mechanics?"

Two men in grease-stained coveralls ran to the jeep, yanked open the hood.

Kirk paced restlessly while the mechanics chattered in Portuguese and tinkered with the engine.

Ten minutes passed. Several more attempts were made to start the vehicle. Kirk lit a cigarette, took one puff, angrily ground it in the dust under his boot, then lit another and did the same to it.

Finally, the jeep engine spluttered to life.

"All right, people," the A.D. yelled through his bullhorn. "This time it's a take."

He handed the horn to the interpreter who repeated his words in Portuguese.

Film was racing through the cameras as the jeep took off in a fresh hail of special effects gunfire. Squibs planted along the street and in the adobe walls of the little deserted village exploded in puffs of dust, simulating bullets striking all around the wildly careening jeep. More charges of dynamite were set off to indicate the explosion of mortar fire. At one spot a dynamite charge was timed to go off as the rear wheels of the jeep raced over it. The force of the explosion hurled the jeep several feet into the air. For a frightening moment, it looked as if the vehicle would flip over, but the highly skilled stunt driver behind the wheel managed to regain control. The jeep slithered and spun around, then righted itself and continued its final dash out of the village into a jungle road.

At Kirk's signal, the assistant director called, "All right. That's a take. No more for today, people."

After washing the dust and perspiration of the morning's work away in an improvised outdoor shower made private by canvas walls, Natalie changed into a clean shirt and jeans. She crossed a clearing to the tent that she had shared with Ginny for the past two weeks.

They were surrounded on all sides by tropical vegetation growing in uncontrolled profusion. Giant roots were smothered by plants and vines that writhed around each other in a perpetual embrace. Tree branches had furry coatings of green moss. Vines as thick as Natalie's wrist festooned the tree branches, dangling to the ground.

It was a world saturated with the color green except for the brilliant hues of tropical flowers. Fragile orchids grew wild in the trees among clusters of bamboo, brilliant red bougainvillaeas, passionflowers, tree ferns, trumpet trees and Brazilian spider flower trees. Begonia blossoms created brilliant yellow splashes with their blossoms among the sago palms, jacarandas and lobsterclaws. There were great wild fruit trees like the jackfruit tree with its enormous thirty-pound fruits.

Parrots adorned with yellow, green and purple feathers flittered through the trees. Monkeys hung by their tails, chattering and jeering at Natalie as she passed. She laughed and made faces back at them.

It was both beautiful and dangerous. They had been warned of the death that lurked in the branches, such as the jararaca snakes, whose fangs carried a deadly venom.

Attempts had been made to give them a few civilized comforts. Gasoline generators ran day and night supplying power to the camp and providing electricity to run air-conditioners that kept some of the jungle heat and molding dampness out of the tents.

When Natalie entered the tent she found her cousin, Ginny Wells, sprawled on a cot, looking utterly exhausted.

"Thank heaven this is over!" Ginny said with a great sigh.

"You did a fantastic job with all the effects, Ginny," Natalie exclaimed, sitting on the other cot.

"I've been scared spitless the entire time. I just knew somebody was going to get an arm or leg blown off. D'you know that maniac, Kirk, had a thousand pounds of dynamite flown up here? The whole camp could have gone sky high any minute."

Natalie shuddered.

The past several weeks had been a nightmare. First there had been the bitter conflict with the studio over Kirk's demands for extra financing and shooting time. Kasserman had flatly refused. There had been a lot of furious yelling over long-distance telephone lines. Kirk decided to fly to Los Angeles for a face-to-face confrontation. He pleaded with Natalie to go with him. "I can't get anywhere with that blockhead," he said. "Maybe he'll listen to you."

At first Natalie refused. "It's not my place to get

involved in this, Kirk. You're the producer and director."

"But we're all in this together. It's our production company. You have a stake in it, too," he argued. "And you have more influence with the studio than any of the rest of us. They won't listen to Ginny or the Dentmens or me. All the other people down here like Howard Ansco—that assistant producer they hung around my neck—are studio stooges. They're siding with Kasserman. Please go with me, Natalie."

Furious with herself for giving in to Kirk again, she had thrown a few things into a bag and let him drive her to the airport. On the flight to Los Angeles, she had refused to sit with Kirk or even speak to him. When the plane landed, she took a separate car home and avoided Kirk until the conference at Sam Kasserman's office.

It had been an angry meeting. Kirk presented a strong argument for the scenes he wanted added to the film. Kasserman was stubborn, not wanting to commit the studio to a larger budget.

Natalie finally broke the deadlock by taking sides with Kirk, pursuading the studio head that the added scenes could result in a much stronger, more suspenseful story, giving it the added global political impact that Kirk was striving for. "It's a big picture, Sam," Natalie said. "It doesn't make sense to pinch pennies when we're aiming at such high stakes."

"Pennies!" Kasserman laughed bitterly. "Natalie, honey, we're not talking pennies; we're talking millions. New York is going to ask a lot of questions about this."

His fingers drummed nervously on the vast expanse

of his bare mahogany desk as he wrestled inwardly
with the problem.

Natalie felt a wave of sympathy for the embattled
studio head. She knew he was in a precarious position, balancing the prospects of a big box office
success against millions of dollars of the studio's
money. It was the biggest kind of high-stakes dice roll
in the world.

Finally he threw his hands up in a gesture of
surrender. "I'm probably cutting my own throat. But
you'd better bring this thing in on schedule, Kirk.
You've already got shooting time to make up."

"Don't worry, Sam," Kirk said confidently.

"Hah! Don't worry, he says!"

Transporting an entire film production crew including the cast, extras and equipment by helicopter and
primitive mountain roads to the remote jungle location had been a monumental undertaking. There had
been endless problems involving supplies, hiring local
extras, dealing with labor unions. Nothing had gone
right. Equipment had broken down and had to be
flown into Rio for repairs. There had been a tropical
rainfall that lasted the better part of a week, delaying
them further. They were bitten by insects, tortured by
the heat, frightened by jungle snakes.

The only good thing Natalie could admit to was that
the scenery was breathtaking. She envisioned the
audience impact of the sweeping panorama of jungle-
covered mountains on a wide screen.

Now the last foot of film at this location had been
shot.

"Well," Ginny said, "with this out of the way, I'll

be flying back to Los Angeles. Why don't you come with me, Natalie?"

"I might do that," Natalie replied thoughtfully. "The scenes Kirk is going to be shooting in Tunis for the next several weeks will involve Tom Sacks and Marsha Sanders. He doesn't need me there. I thought I'd either spend some time in New York or Los Angeles before going on to Tunisia."

"Come back with me," Ginny urged. "We both need to get out of this jungle and go on a shopping spree."

"That sounds enticing. You're about to convince me."

"I hope I can. I'd like to show you what we've done on the outer space sets."

"Yes, I would like to see those. I'm always fascinated by the magic you special effects experts can create. There seems to be no end to your ingenuity."

"If I have any ingenuity, Kirk is making me stretch it to the limits," Ginny muttered. "He never does anything on a modest scale!"

"I know. This picture is going to have some staggering visual effects if he pulls it off."

"Also a staggering budget! With the equipment breakdowns, the delays the rains caused and the other problems we ran into up here, he's fallen even further behind the shooting schedule. The cost here ran way over the studio's projections. And some of the most expensive stuff is yet to be made, the space station scenes and the action episodes in Tunisia."

Natalie agreed, a worried expression crossing her face. She was growing increasingly alarmed at the way

Kirk was handling the finances. He was doing exactly what the studio feared, ignoring budget limitations, doing things his own way and hang the cost.

"Have you tried talking him into holding down the expenses?" Ginger asked.

Natalie laughed shortly. "Nobody can tell Kirk anything about how to shoot a film, Ginger. You know that."

"What if the studio gets cold feet and pulls the rug out from under us? It wouldn't be the first time that's happened to a producer, you know."

"I know. But at this point we can just hold our breath and hope they'll decide that since they've invested this much, they might as well spend a little more."

They were busy the rest of the morning with packing.

Early that afternoon, they walked to the clearing where the helicopter was waiting to fly them back to civilization. Kirk was there, overseeing the loading of cans filled with exposed film.

He greeted Ginny and Natalie. "I guess I won't be seeing you two ladies for a few weeks."

"Right," Ginger said. "Natalie is going to Los Angeles with me to see how the sets on the sound stages are coming along."

"Good." He nodded. "Let me know how things look there."

His hazel eyes turned toward Natalie. She felt the familiar surge of adrenaline as her pulse quickened. Would she ever be strong enough to ignore the effect his intense gaze could have on her?

"I'm going to need both of you in Tunisia in a few weeks," he reminded them.

"Yes," Ginger said. "The sets you're planning to construct in the desert."

"Correct. We'll need some more of your expertise for that. Right now, though, we'll be doing some scenes in Tunis, where the Russian agent, Nichole Nikova, enters the story and contacts Clay Winters. That will take up all our time for a while and will give you a breathing spell."

Natalie tried to be cool and distant as she nodded briefly and walked past him. But inwardly her emotions were a battleground.

Kirk touched her arm as she moved by him. The contact was electrifying. Her knees suddenly became watery.

He captured her arm and turned her deliberately around to face him. Her eyes were wide, the pupils expanding over the irises.

His gaze was filled with a strange, burning intensity that sapped the strength from her body and made her legs tremble. Why was he looking at her in this way, she asked herself out of the whirlwind of emotions that his look had created. What did it mean? Was he thinking about that night on the yacht?

"See you in Tunisia," he murmured.

Suddenly, without warning, he bent and his lips brushed hers.

She pulled away from him, totally disoriented. She fled to the helicopter. Her lips burned from the kiss. She was breathing hard, furious at her traitorous emotions. What good did it do to swear to herself she would keep her emotional distance from Kirk until this film was completed when she reacted like this?

When the whirling blades lifted them skyward, she looked down. Kirk was standing there, legs apart, hands on hips, gazing up at them. His words echoed in her mind. "See you in Tunisia. . . ."

They were halfway back to Rio before the trembling inside her subsided.

Chapter Thirteen

ℐou can boil down the whole business of special effects into three categories. First, you don't have to run film through the camera continuously. You can photograph each frame separately, then project it at a normal speed. Second, you can 'fake' reality with various kinds of artwork and models that look like the real thing on the screen. And third, you can combine one or more images onto one strip of film. You can bet the effects you've seen from a Walt Disney cartoon to *Star Wars* use one or all of those techniques."

Ginny Wells was discussing her craft as she and Natalie escorted Marie Taylor, a magazine writer, through the sound stages where her crews were hard at work on the sets for the outer space scenes to be used in *The Last Encounter*.

Two weeks had passed since Natalie and Ginny

returned to Los Angeles. It had given Natalie an emotional breathing spell. She had slept late, had gone on shopping trips with Ginny, read and watched TV and tried to forget about what lay ahead of her in Tunisia.

Yesterday, the studio publicity department had called to let her know that a well-known national magazine, *Persons and Events,* was sending a staff writer around to do an article on *The Last Encounter* production. Natalie knew it was the job of the unit publicist to attract media coverage to a promising release while it was being shot. This usually took the form of on-the-set interviews with directors, writers and stars. Newspaper, TV and magazine journalists were encouraged to make the movie known as early as possible. This publicity was aimed both at the public and at the theater owners who keep close tabs on advance coverage. If the advance media coverage made the film look good to the theater owners it would be easier for the distributor to sell it once it was released.

The writer, Marie Taylor, a bright young woman in her late twenties, was fascinated with the making of movie magic through special effects. Artists, technicians and workmen were busy on projects ranging from interiors of the gigantic space station to miniature models of space shuttles.

"I've been a movie fan all my life," she told Natalie and Ginny. "I've just been amazed at the marvelous things you people get on the screen—the animation, the weird creatures, the scenes in outer space. I was really delighted when I got this assignment so I could see firsthand what goes on behind the scenes."

They stopped at the coffee shop. As they sipped drinks, Ginny continued detailing how effects were achieved, explaining all the different techniques.

All too soon, Marie turned to Natalie. "I'd like to have your feeling about this production, Miss Brooks. How does it feel to be working with your husband?"

The question took Natalie by surprise. She thought, with a bit of irritation, it might be a deliberate trick of a skilled interviewer to catch the subject off guard. She paused to regain her composure and tried to keep her voice level. "I'm afraid I don't exactly understand your question, Miss Taylor."

"Forgive me if I'm getting onto personal ground, but it's common knowledge that you and Kirk Trammer have been estranged for the past two years. Now he's your director. Does that present a problem?"

Natalie frowned. "The production has nothing to do with our personal lives. Kirk is a brilliant director. I respect him professionally as he respects me professionally."

"He has a reputation for being difficult, if not impossible, on the set," Ms. Taylor suggested.

"That's one of those things that's blown out of proportion. Kirk is demanding because he is striving for perfection. He won't hesitate to shoot a scene over a dozen or more times until he gets what he wants."

"Is that why he's known as an expensive producer?"

"Maybe," Natalie said testily. The interview was beginning to stretch her nerves.

"This is apparently going to be a very costly movie. You're filming a lot of scenes on location. You've just come back from Brazil. Where will you be going next?"

"We're flying to Tunisia next week. Ginny will be going there, too. Kirk plans to use the arid, desert setting. He's got a crew out there now, building a mock-up Middle-Eastern village that will play an important part in the story. There's a lot of cliff-hanger action in the movie, chase scenes, shoot-outs, along with a great love story and the international intrigue."

"Would you describe *The Last Encounter* as an action-adventure story, in the James Bond tradition?"

"It's a kind of mixture of romance, science fiction, and intrigue. There is a lot of action and a strong romantic involvement. But it's going to have more substance than just that. Kirk is going to give it an underlying philosophical-political message."

"Which is?"

"That where ideals, politics and philosophy have all failed to eliminate the plague of war, science will eventually provide the key. But there is still the underlying battle between good and evil in human nature that can threaten the peace science has achieved."

The journalist made one of her disconcerting, abrupt subject changes.

"How do you like having Tom Sacks as your screen lover?"

"I enjoy working with Mr. Sacks, if that's what you mean. This part is going to give him a chance to show what a fine actor he really is."

"Yes, but on a personal level. Tom Sacks is probably the most gorgeous hunk on the screen today. Any chance of a real romance developing between the two of you?"

Natalie felt her cheeks color. She thought about that morning on the beach in Rio. Tom was definitely interested in her. But she doubted if she could have any clear feelings on the matter until she knew she was no longer Kirk's wife.

She ducked the writer's question by replying, "There are no men in my life right now. I'm too busy with my role in the film, which is very demanding."

Ms. Taylor tried to pursue the matter of Tom Sacks, but Natalie refused to say any more. The interview was upsetting. As a matter of public relations, she had to be pleasant to the magazine writer, but she was relieved when it was over.

At the end of the week, Natalie left for Tunisia alone. Ginny had run into problems with the sets and had to remain in Los Angeles a few more days.

In the airport, Natalie checked her baggage. Then she stopped at a magazine stand.

Suddenly a picture on the cover of a tabloid leaped out at her. It was one of the sensational weekly publications that specialized in Hollywood gossip. The picture that had riveted her attention was of Kirk and Marsha Sanders in a night club.

The headline read, "Marsha Sanders Once Again Romancing Her Director."

Natalie reached for the publication with trembling fingers, her stomach suddenly in a painful knot. Through angry tears, she read the story written in lurid tabloid style. "They're at it again. When Marsha Sanders starred in *The Two of Us,* she and director,

Kirk Trammer, turned the behind-the-scenes action into their own romantic twosome. Now she's again one of the stars in Trammer's big blockbuster, *The Last Encounter,* currently being filmed on location in Tunisia, and she and the controversial director are writing their own version of the love story. They have been making the rounds of colorful Tunis. Our photographer caught them holding hands in one of the romantic nightclubs. We're definitely in love, Marsha confided to our reporter. I've never been happier in my life. Meanwhile, Kirk's wife, Natalie Brooks, the real star of the film, seems to be out of the picture as far as Trammer's personal life is concerned."

Cold fury whipped through Natalie. She looked down at her left hand. In spite of the impending divorce, she hadn't been able to bring herself to take off her wedding ring. It was the symbol of too many sentimental memories.

Now, she jerked it from her finger as if it were burning her skin. "Well, this does it! So much for you, Kirk Trammer. You're out of my life forever. Good riddance!"

Chapter Fourteen

$\mathcal{T}$unisia . . .

Natalie sat in the improvised projection room in the building rented by the production company in Tunis. The room was small and stifling. But she was unaware of her discomfort. Her entire attention was captured by the images flashed on the screen. These were the rushes of scenes that had been filmed in the narrow, exotic streets of Tunis during her absence. Marsha Sanders was in every scene. Her haunting, dark beauty dominated the screen. She was a gorgeous young woman who photographed exquisitely, Natalie admitted with a deep, wrenching pain. It was easy to see why she and Kirk had become lovers.

The screen glared white as the last frame was flipped through the projector. Kirk, who had been sitting beside her, rose and switched on the lights.

"Well, what do you think of them?" he asked.

"They look good," Natalie said stiffly.

Marsha, playing the lovely Russian agent, Nichole Nikova, had entered the story at this point and had become involved with the American hero, Clay Winters, creating the love triangle with Natalie's Rebecca Abrahms. *In the movie, just like in real life, she's trying to take my man away,* Natalie thought wryly.

She gazed at Kirk, feeling a mixture of anger and pain. The last thing she had expected was for Kirk to meet her plane when she landed at Tunis. "Why are you here?" she'd demanded at the airport.

He'd shrugged. "Somebody had to meet you. You'd be lost in this city. Everyone else in the production company has moved out to the desert location. I just came into the city to look over some rushes. I'll take you to your hotel, but first I want to stop off and see what those scenes we filmed last week look like."

The lurid tabloid story about Kirk and Marsha was smoldering in her handbag. But as angry as she was, she couldn't stifle the physical awareness of his presence. The taxi had seemed filled with the heat from his body. No matter how much she seethed with anger at his betrayal, the hunger for him remained.

Now after viewing the rushes with him, she couldn't keep the edge out of her voice as she said, "Marsha looks beautiful. You know just what camera angle to use with her."

Kirk nodded absently. "She's fine in that part. I knew she would be." Then he said, "Come on, let's get something to eat."

She wanted to cut him short, to plead a headache and go straight to her hotel room. But the traitorous emotions that clamored to be near him were too strong. It made her wonder at her own sanity. How could she experience the way he'd hurt her and still have these mixed emotions—the ambivalence that made her hate him and desire him at the same time? Was love that closely related to hate?

She had to dismiss the impulse to touch his hand, to reach up and brush her fingers through his thick hair. She struggled to keep fantasies of them in bed together from surging through her mind, making her heart pound and her breasts ache.

Would she ever get over this irresistible physical attraction for him that enslaved her in such a devastating manner?

Yearning for him was a dead-end street. It lead to nowhere but a futile wall of heartache. He didn't love her; he had never loved her. It was impossible to build a marriage on those sad terms.

She cursed herself for her weakness even as she gathered up her purse and let him escort her out of the building to a taxi.

The general architecture of Tunis gave the city the appearance of being low and white. Most of the buildings in the modern section were not over six or seven stories tall. As they drove along the Avenue Habib Bourguiba, they passed the municipal theater, banks and main hotels. They made a stop at one of the hotels where Kirk registered for her and had her bags sent to her room. Then, following Kirk's order, the driver of their cab picked his way through the heavy traffic of the broad main streets and turned into the narrow, winding alleyways of the old city, al-Madinah. Natalie felt as if they had left the twentieth century behind. In this Muslim section were clustered the bazaars, the individual markets called "sugs," dating back to the Hafsid dynasty of the middle ages. On display were handcrafted carpets, pottery, leather and intricately carved silver and gold jewelry. Shopkeepers hawked their wares in singsong Arabic voices.

Here in this medieval city, the narrow streets wound among one-story, ancient, windowless houses that resembled white cubes. Time seemed suspended here, as if it were still eight centuries before Christ, when Phoenician merchants founded the city of Carthage here on the Mediterranean coast.

The weight of centuries rested on this most ancient of cities. In the dust of ages, Natalie felt the presence of lingering ghosts, the Vandals, Arabs and Turks—all conquerers of Carthage. The sandaled footsteps of Roman centurions seemed to echo down the corridors of the alleys. Twice Carthage had been sacked and burned. Twice it had risen from the ashes.

"I found this little café run by a French couple," Kirk said. "We've become good friends. They have a piano and I'd come down here and have a bottle of wine and play at night when we finished filming for the day."

That was Kirk's style. Natalie knew him so well. Wherever he went, he managed to find some little family-owned café that became his temporary home.

"Arabic is the official language of Tunisia," Kirk went on, "but a lot of French is spoken. It was a French protectorate from 1881 until 1956. French is still very prominent in the press, in education and in the government. You should have no trouble with the language."

When they stepped out of the cab, Natalie drew her coat collar closer. There was a faint, cold mist in the air. This time of the year, the Mediterranean climate was cool and damp along the northern coast.

They entered a narrow doorway, stepped down a short flight of stairs and entered a small room containing no more than a half dozen tables covered with red checkered cloths. The lighting was soft. Only two other couples were eating dinner.

A short, bald man greeted Kirk profusely in English with a thick Gallic accent and gave him an impulsive embrace.

Kirk patted his shoulder, winking at Natalie. "It took a while but I've managed to talk him out of kissing me on the cheek." Then to the café owner, "Monsieur Petreaux, this is my wife, Natalie Brooks."

The roly-poly café owner beamed, clasping his hands in ecstasy. "Ah, Natalie Brooks, ze mos' famous, beautiful American movie star. I 'ave seen all your pictures. You 'ave done me ze great honor to come to my humble café!" Then he called to the kitchen. "Mama! Come quick!" And there followed a barrage of excited French.

Remembering her finishing school French, Natalie picked out enough words to know that she had become the center of attention in the small café. She was thankful that more customers were not present. She was embraced by Madame Petreaux, who was as plump and jolly as her husband. The two couples who were dining in the small café left their tables to gaze at her in awe and requested that she autograph their menus. One of them had a camera. Natalie had to oblige everyone by being photographed with each person present as they took turns operating the camera.

At last, she and Kirk were escorted to a table in a secluded corner and the other customers returned to their meals, too excited to notice the food had grown cold.

The café owner brought Natalie and Kirk a bottle of his best wine and promised an unforgettable meal. He made a parting gesture, kissing his fingers, then scurrying to the kitchen to help his wife with the meal.

Kirk raised his wineglass, looking moodily at Natalie. There was an edge in his voice as he said, "Well, shall we drink to our divorce?"

"I don't think that's exactly something to be toasted," she replied coldly.

He raised an eyebrow. "Well, then, here's to having you back."

Her lips tightened. "I doubt if you even noticed I was gone. Surely your mistress kept you occupied."

His reply was a dark frown. "What are you talking about?"

Natalie took the folded tabloid article from her handbag and flung it on the table.

He glanced at it, then chuckled. "Oh, that."

"Yes, that. You don't waste any time, do you? You can't even wait until our divorce is final before you begin squiring your girl friend around in public."

"You may be jumping to conclusions. Who says Marsha is my girl friend?"

By way of reply, Natalie pointed to the tabloid article. "She seems to think so."

"Natalie," Kirk said, with a note of exasperation, "surely you of all people wouldn't be so naïve as to believe one of these scandal sheets. You know half the people in the entertainment industry are suing these tabloids for distortions and lies."

"The picture is clear enough. Do you deny being out with her?"

"Well, what did you expect me to do, stay home and knit?" he snapped angrily. "You're off in Los Angeles divorcing me. What am I supposed to do? It gets lonesome in the evenings."

Natalie shrugged. "Of course you have every right to do whatever you want, see whomever you want. Why should I care? After all, you were involved with her long before I filed for divorce."

Kirk sighed. "Marsha, Tom Sacks and I went out to eat dinner one night to discuss some scenes we were working on. I remember a camera flashing once when Tom left the table for some reason. That's probably when that picture was taken."

She gave him a long, puzzled look. Why was he trying to convince her?

"If you don't believe me, ask Tom Sacks," he persisted.

"I think I'd rather ask Marsha Sanders," Natalie countered. "She's the one who told the reporter, 'We're definitely in love,' to quote the article."

Kirk shrugged in a noncommittal manner. "I have no control over what Marsha says—if, indeed, she did say it." He left it at that and drank his wine in brooding silence.

Natalie realized for the first time how tired he looked. There were dark circles under his eyes and lines of tension around his mouth. She remembered how he could throw himself into his work with such intensity that he went without sleep for days. She realized he looked exhausted, almost ill. Some of her own anger began to melt. She felt something inside her soften.

"You—you look tired," she began hesitantly. "Aren't things going well?"

"No, they're not going well. As a matter of fact, everything is going wrong. We've gotten way behind schedule. We're running into all kinds of problems out in the desert, sand storms, malfunctions. Half the crew is down with one ailment or another."

An unexpected wave of sympathy swept over her. Feeling contrite for giving him such a bad time since stepping off the plane, she reached across the table and clasped his hand. "Kirk, I'm sorry. I didn't realize things had gotten so desperate."

Her gaze roamed over his tired, care-worn features and the softness grew inside until it caught at her breath. The urge to brush her fingers over the lines around his lips, to kiss the tension and worry away, was almost more than she could bear. "How bad is it, Kirk?"

"It could be the end of the production."

"Oh, Kirk!" Now she felt her blood run cold.

He nodded. "You know the studio reluctantly agreed to the original budget. All the indications now are that it's going to cost at least ten million more to finish this thing. That two-faced little assistant producer they hung around my neck sneaked some rushes back to Sam Kasserman and he's screaming bloody murder."

"Ansco had no business doing that!"

"Of course not! What can Kasserman tell from

some unedited roughs? Nevertheless, he didn't like what he saw. And with the shooting falling so far behind schedule, the cost escalating—" He shook his head. "I'm afraid they're going to pull the rug out from under us, Natalie."

She hardly knew what to say. She didn't have the heart to remind him that the executives at Continental Films had warned Kirk from the beginning that his reputation for ignoring budget limitations could get him in trouble. She could only hold onto his hand as if to keep him from drowning. Forgotten for the moment were all the emotions of bitterness, anger and hurt that had dominated her heart a few minutes ago. They seemed petty in comparison to the crisis Kirk was facing.

"What are you going to do?" she asked.

He shrugged with a helpless expression. "Keep on shooting until they pull the plug, I guess. Maybe we can get the desert shots on film."

"But you haven't started on the space scenes. The sets aren't even finished."

"I know. It doesn't look good, unless we can get more financing."

"Kirk, I don't know what to say. It's a terrific motion picture. Whatever personal problems we've had, I never had a single doubt about this being the big picture of the year. They just can't shelve it."

He smiled wryly. "Want to bet?"

No, she didn't want to bet, she thought with a feeling of despair. It wouldn't be the first production to be canceled because of a budget that had grown out of control.

"Something is festering at the studio. I'm not sure

what," he said. "I'm just getting rumors out here. I think there's going to be a shake-up. You know David Clawson, the head executive of the parent corporation in New York, has been after Sam Kasserman's scalp for some time. He might be using this film to get Sam replaced as head of the studio. He wants somebody he can control. As soon as that happens, *The Last Encounter* is going to be shelved. You can depend on that. Or, Kasserman might shelve it first to save his own hide. Right now this film project is extremely unpopular both at Continental Films and the parent corporation in New York. The consensus of opinion seems to be that it's turning into a costly disaster."

"The publicity department had a writer from *Persons and Events* on the sets just before I left," Natalie told him. "Do you think they'd be publicizing a film that's going to be shelved?"

"It hasn't filtered down to the lower executives and departments yet. From the rumors I'm getting, this is a struggle going on at the highest management level. Could even be something the board of directors at Atlantic Enterprises is fighting over. You have a great-uncle on that board. Have you heard anything I don't know?"

She shook her head. "I haven't been to New York since we started shooting this film. I spent the last three weeks in Hollywood with Ginny."

The meal came. The French dishes were delicious, prepared with loving care, but Natalie had lost her appetite. She forced herself to eat, not wanting to hurt the café owner's feelings. He bustled around their table like an anxious parent, making sure everything was perfect.

After the meal, Monsieur Petreaux asked Kirk if he would play the piano. "He has so much talent," he said to Natalie. "Last night he played the *Marseillaise*. I cried."

The café owner bustled off to fetch them a fresh bottle of wine as Kirk moved to a piano bar set up at the other side of the room. Natalie took a seat, watching Kirk's strong fingers race over the keyboard. She understood Monsieur Petreaux's emotions. More than once Kirk had made her cry with his melodies. Tonight, she was very close to tears, swamped with a thousand bittersweet memories as the wreckage of a broken marriage lay at her feet.

She sensed from the kind of selections Kirk played as his fingers roamed the keyboard, that he, too, was caught up in a sentimental mood. Was he remembering the times they had laughed together, cried together, fought and made up? Did he feel any regrets? Or was he relieved to be getting out of a marriage that had meant so little to him?

Monsieur Petreaux reappeared from the wine cellar. "This is a special occasion," he said, proudly placing a bottle on the piano bar with fresh glasses. "Our best Napoleon brandy."

Kirk smiled and broke into a strain from the *Marseillaise*. The rotund café owner stood proudly at attention, tears filling his eyes.

As Kirk continued to play, straying from one melody to another, Natalie realized more people were drifting into the café and gathering around the piano. She decided this must have become a regular nightly event while Kirk was filming the street scenes in Tunis. He had attracted something of a following.

Tonight word had spread that he was in town for the evening and his friends had come to hear him. He played popular French tunes and they sang, and he played American show tunes and love ballads, and he played Chopin and Tchaikovsky and Cole Porter and Burt Bacharach. His mood ranged from sentimental to sad to brave to angry. He played like a man obsessed.

Natalie thought that for Kirk, the piano was a form of therapy, a means of emotional catharsis, where he could relieve the anger and tension and frustration that was tearing him apart.

When he played like this, Natalie came closer to understanding this complex man who had been her husband and her lover than at any other time. There were sides to Kirk that had forever remained a mystery to her. Perhaps that had been the fatal flaw in their marriage—the fact that she had never really known Kirk Trammer. Though they made love and slept together, they had remained strangers. She had intuitively sensed that he was a man living with some kind of relentless inner torment. Was it the grief and guilt over the accident that killed Jacqueline Davis, the woman he'd loved? Was it the emotional scars left over from war? Was it the inner, driving torment that often haunted and pursued creative people?

Whatever it was, Kirk had never been able to talk about it with her. Some parts of his inner being, he kept behind locked doors. He held her at a distance. But when he played the way he did tonight, she caught glimpses of those emotions he kept under wraps.

Natalie was oblivious to the passage of time. It grew very late. Monsieur Petreaux closed the café, locking the front door, but the group around the piano remained. Perhaps it was the Napoleon brandy she sipped or Kirk's music or the emotional wasteland left behind by their broken marriage, but she felt detached from reality. In the small, smoke-filled room, the ceiling fan slowly turning overhead, the music made her feel that she was in a scene from *Casablanca,* filmed through a soft, hazy lens.

It was very late, long past midnight, when Kirk wearily rose from the piano. His friends crowded around him, shaking his hand and embracing him, and they all drifted out into the chilly Mediterranean night. The mist had turned into softly falling rain. Natalie shivered as the drops touched her cheeks.

In the taxi, it seemed natural that she would sit close to Kirk and be warmed by his strong arm. She rested her head on his shoulder as she had done so many times in the past. She was still in the dreamlike state, detached from reality. Dimly, she realized that the legal process of filing for a divorce decree did not automatically turn off patterns of physical response. Her body was ignoring the decree, fitting itself closer to his, following a comfortable habit of intimacy.

Words were not spoken or needed. Kirk's lips found hers. His hand moved under her dress, sliding up her inner thighs in a familiar caress that heated her deep inside and brought a quickened tempo to her breathing. For this moment, she seemed unable to remember that their marriage was ending. This coming together, this giving of her intimacy to his caresses was such a normal response that she could not find the strength to deny it, nor did she want to. Forgotten for now was the anger, the bitterness, the estrangement.

Passion was raging through her veins, demanding satisfaction from this man who, in spite of everything, could still excite her so.

Years ago, she had given her virginity to Kirk. There had been no man before him. He had been the one to awaken her to a woman's passion. And she had shared no other man's bed since she'd known Kirk. Why wouldn't her body seek his for fulfillment?

Her lips responded to his hungrily. Her hands roamed over him as his did over hers. She felt his muscles, his hardness, and her breath strained in her throat. She slid her fingers under his shirt over his chest, plowing through the mat of crisp, curly hair at the same time that his hand found her breast under her blouse and cupped the round softness there.

She felt as eager as a bride when the taxi brought them to her hotel. "Hurry," she whispered shamelessly.

Then they were in her room, again locked in each other's arms. The only light came from the soft glow of a single lamp.

They stood kissing as their clothes fell in a heap at their feet. Kirk scooped her in his arms and carried her to the bed. Her bare flesh against his burned as if with a high fever. She groaned with pleasure as his weight bore down on her. Her arms and legs were locked around him in a straining embrace as they kissed feverishly.

"Oh, Kirk," she moaned. "Oh . . . oh . . . oh—"

She gave herself to him with total abandon as never before.

The hours passed. Through the windows dawn

began to tinge the eastern sky. Passion spent at last, Natalie slept peacefully.

Kirk sat by the window, smoking a cigarette and gazing moodily at his wife's profile, soft and lovely in repose.

It had happened again, he thought with a sense of bitter frustration. Natalie had come to him tonight, not out of respect and love but out of pity, just like that night in Malibu. She had felt sorry for him because of the disaster that was looming over the production like a black cloud.

He was sure that the last thing she had expected or wanted was to sleep with Kirk Trammer ever again. Once again he had caught her in a vulnerable mood. She'd had no sex since that night on the beach at Malibu, months ago. She had been love starved. Her emotions had been swamped by the pending divorce. Everything had conspired against her—the compassion for Kirk because of the strain he was under, the sentimental mood his music had evoked, the brandy she had sipped, the romance of the ancient, exotic city.

But tonight's interlude, lovely as it was, had solved none of their problems.

Their situation was by no means unique. They wouldn't be the first couple to get a divorce because of their careers. Numerous well-known Hollywood marriages had gone on the rocks because the wife's acting career blossomed into stardom while the husband went through a period of failure.

He had made a vow that he was not going to make

another attempt to touch Natalie unless the picture was a success. Now that possibility was becoming more remote by the day. He felt like a condemned man going through the motions of directing the film as he waited for the ax to fall.

The next morning, they flew by helicopter to the desert location in the southern part of Tunisia. The set was a mocked-up Middle-Eastern village built in the rocky desert terrain by a crew Kirk had working overtime.

There for the next several weeks, Kirk drove the production company relentlessly, shooting scenes from the first light of day to the last without a day off. It was as if he were in a desperate race to shoot every foot of film he possibly could while there was yet time.

Ginny and her crew worked under lights at night to get the special effects paraphernalia set up for the following day.

As in the Central American sequence, there was a lot of dangerous stunt work, buildings blown apart, tanks rumbling through the rubble.

There was a scene in which terrorists had torched an American embassy building. Ginny had the problem of creating the effect of the building being on fire. She used a portable, fire breathing machine patterned after one devised by a British special effects expert, Cliff Richardson. The machine built by Richardson and his son consisted of a Volkswagen motor and a pump mounted on a two-wheeled carriage. They had given it the suitable name of the "Dante." Ginny had made some modifications of the original idea.

When the machine was turned on, the pumping

machinery sent fuel surging up jets set behind windows and on the roof. Flames forty feet high leaped from the roof and out of windows. Paraffin was used for fuel because it was safer to work with than gasoline.

Chemicals were mixed with the fuel to color the flames so they would show up more vividly. Ordinary flames would appear almost transparent when filmed.

The effect was dramatic as stunt people wearing fire-protective material under their clothes and oxygen supplies under face masks stumbled out of the building ablaze from head to foot. And at the same time, tanks rumbled around a corner, blasting away with cannons and machine guns.

Tempers grew short. The cast was near exhaustion. "The man is insane," Tom Sacks muttered angrily. "How long does he think we can keep up this pace?"

The answer came in the form of a telegram from the office of the head of Continental Films.

"Stop all work on *The Last Encounter* immediately. Decision made to suspend production on the film."

Chapter Fifteen

New York and Hollywood . . . It was the end.

The equipment was dismantled. The production crew was paid off and sent home. Natalie's last hope for her marriage dissolved with the dust of the desert they left behind.

After that night of passion in Kirk's arms in Tunis, she'd wondered if a miracle might yet save their marriage. That night proved again that whatever other problems they had, the bedroom was not one of them. But when they flew to the desert location, Kirk had gone back to treating her with cold indifference. And when word came from the studio that the film had been canceled, Kirk hadn't even said good-bye. He handled the details of dismantling production and then simply disappeared without a word to her.

She wasn't surprised. It only confirmed what she

had believed all along—that Kirk's only interest in her was as a ticket to studio backing of his production. With that gone, he had no further use for her.

But she still had a vital interest in the film. Her closest friends were involved. They had all invested months of hard work in this motion picture. They were crushed by this cruel turn of events. Their dreams of a successful production company were shattered.

Natalie returned to New York, determined to uncover the reason production had been canceled. She felt convinced there was more behind the act than budget problems. There was some kind of intrigue boiling at the corporate level.

Once settled in her New York apartment, she made some phone calls and discovered that Sam Kasserman had flown in from the West Coast. She began by cornering him in his hotel suite.

She saw at once the strain the motion picture executive was under. It was a different Sam Kasserman from the imperious studio head who sat behind his desk like it was a throne. He looked haggard and tired. His usually immaculate attire was slightly rumpled. He moved around the room, his hands twitching slightly as he touched various objects. When Natalie tried to pin him down, he was evasive.

"What can I tell you, Natalie? The cost overrun was getting out of hand. We had to call a halt to Kirk's extravagance. It had gotten to be too big a gamble—"

"But you believed in the story."

"Yes, it's a good script. But it's costing too much."

"Sam, you can't do this kind of big motion picture

for small change anymore. You know that. I think you're throwing away a chance to make millions for the studio."

Kasserman made a helpless gesture. "It's out of my hands, Natalie."

"Out of my hands—" In that phrase, Natalie had a clue as to what was happening.

She called David Clawson, chief executive officer of the Atlantic Enterprises corporation. He suggested they have lunch at "21."

Natalie often thought that if she were casting the part of a successful corporate executive approaching middle age, she would pick David Clawson. He would be typecast in the role of a forceful, self-assured executive. His walk was brisk. He stood erect. His penetrating blue eyes were unwavering. More than one board member's gaze had faltered under that piercing look. His movements were deliberate and precise and his soft, well-modulated voice carried an undercurrent of firm authority.

At forty-five, his light brown hair had a few strands of gray at the temples. His favorite dishes of Maine lobster, top sirloin and imported wines had given him a well-fed, slightly fleshy look around the cheeks and neck, but his complexion was kept a healthy pink by hours on the racketball court. His tailored, dark gray suit had an air of subtle elegance. His only jewelry consisted of a pair of gold cuff links and a platinum wristwatch.

Over the meal at "21," they began with an exchange of polite conversation. Natalie asked about his wife and two teenage children. He talked about the last film she'd starred in, *Never Tomorrow,* which was enjoying a profitable run with the promise of future profits down the line with its eventual TV release. He said she should get an Academy Award nomination for her part, which Natalie knew was pure flattery. Nothing about the picture was Academy Award material.

Then Natalie brought the conversation around to the main subject. "David, I'm at a loss to understand why Continental Films has shelved production on *The Last Encounter*."

Clawson looked surprised. He put his fork down and took a sip of wine. "I thought Sam Kasserman made it clear. The cost was getting out of hand."

"But the picture will be worth it—"

Clawson shook his head. "Sam did a real dumb thing, getting into that, Natalie. That project had 'loser' written all over it."

Natalie flushed but made a determined effort to keep her emotions under control. She worked hard to maintain a pleasant front. "Sam has a reputation for being one of the top film executives in Hollywood, David," she said gently. "He thought from the beginning it was a good script. Don't you trust his judgment?"

Clawson smiled, but his eyes were cold. "No, frankly, I don't always trust his judgment, Natalie."

"He's made the studio show a profit, hasn't he?"

A tinge of annoyance glinted in David Clawson's eyes. "That's not the point, Natalie. Sam has become entirely too arrogant. He went ahead with this production over my objections in the first place."

Natalie did not pursue the subject. She had heard enough. The next day she paid her mother an obligatory, long-overdue visit and the following night she went to see her favorite relative, her great-uncle, Jeffrey Brooks, who lived on Long Island.

The patriarch of the Brooks family, approaching seventy, had a mane of white hair, eyes as blue as the sky reflected in a clear pool and a complexion of pure mahogany, carefully cultivated on his sailboat. He stood as erect as a Viking. His greeting was a bear hug and a remonstration for neglecting him.

"I haven't seen you in six months, child!"

"I know, Uncle Jeffrey. Will you forgive me?"

"Well, I don't know. Let's have something to drink while I think about it."

They had snifters of expensive brandy in the luxuriously paneled den of the Long Island mansion.

"Uncle Jeffrey, what is going on at Atlantic Enterprises?" Natalie asked.

"Whatever do you mean, child?" he asked blandly.

"Oh, don't act so innocent," she chided. "I see that twinkle in your eyes. There's something afoot."

"Well, now, what do you think it is?"

"I think David Clawson is out to get Sam Kasserman's scalp, is what I think," she replied. "And the fallout of those two at each other's throat is killing the picture I'm working on."

"Oh, yes. *The Last Encounter*. Your husband's big epic." The blue eyes became penetrating. "How are things with you two, anyway? I hear rumors you are divorcing him."

She flushed. "Yes. But that's another matter."

"Too bad. I hate to see that. Didn't want you to turn into one of those Hollywood types, running from husband to husband."

Her cheeks grew warmer. "It's not like that, Uncle Jeffrey. There . . . there are problems—"

He made a conciliatory gesture. "Now, Natalie sweetheart, don't take offense at an old man who loves you. I know what a difficult thing it is for people in your profession to have any kind of normal home life: the long separations while you're off on location, the volatile nature of talented, creative people, the strain of two careers in the same family, especially when one is successful and one is not."

Natalie frowned and started to reply, but her great-uncle interrupted. "Now, we won't talk about your private life anymore. But I would like to know why you're concerned about the picture. Is it because it's Kirk's production? Because your friends are involved in the production company? Because you have the starring role?"

Natalie sighed. "I suppose it's all of those things. And it's so damned unfair, Uncle Jeffrey! Let's leave Kirk and my friends out of it. And, yes, forget the fact that I had the lead role, which happens to be one of the best I've ever gotten, by the way. Putting all those things aside, I'd still be upset about this because it's a marvelous story. Granted, it's going to cost more to produce than first estimated, and maybe Kirk has rather grandiose ideas that are expensive. But that's what it takes to produce a motion picture of this magnitude. Have you read the script, Uncle Jeffrey?"

"Yes, as a matter of fact, I have. And before you spend any more breath trying to convince me, I'll tell you that I agree with you."

"You do?" she asked with surprise. "I thought

everyone on the board at Atlantic Enterprises was dead set against it.''

"Oh, no. Not by any means. Some of us are a hundred percent behind the production. We think it will be the biggest money-maker Continental Films has ever produced.''

Natalie digested that bit of information in a moment of surprised silence. "Then the fight is between David Clawson and Sam Kasserman?"

"Exactly. And both have strong allies on the board of directors. Natalie, it's not unusual for a corporate executive like David to be attracted to the glamour of the Hollywood scene. He wants to be more directly involved with the allure of movie making. The way he can do that is to get Sam Kasserman out of the way and put his own man at the head of Continental Films. He's using this fight over *The Last Encounter* production to prejudice the board against Sam, trying to convince us that Sam has lost his touch, has done an utterly foolish thing to take on a producer who laid such a bad egg with his last film.

"You see, using his position as the head of Atlantic Enterprises, David could just go ahead and fire Sam. But he's walking a tightrope. That action could backfire and get him fired if the board of directors didn't agree. So David is trying to convince us he's right, to make sure he has a majority of the stockholders behind him when he makes his move to can Sam Kasserman.''

"What are his odds?"

"Pretty nearly even. Now let me ask you this: Do you want to save the production?"

"Of course I do!"

Jeffrey Brooks took a sip of his brandy, his eyes sparkling like bright, blue marbles. "Then, I think you and I should fly down to Miami and have a chat with my old friend, Willie Thompson. Willie is on the board and he's one of the company's biggest stockholders. I suspect that old pirate has been quietly buying up stock here and there, hoping one day to corner controlling interest. Willie and I go a long way back. We were shipmates in the Pacific in '42. If we can get Willie on our side, it might be David who gets the ax instead of Sam."

Natalie grinned. "Uncle Jeffrey, you rascal, you like a good fight. You're enjoying all this!"

"Maybe." Then he winked. "Willie still likes to look at a pretty girl, so cross your legs and bat those long, gorgeous eyelashes at him."

"Uncle Jeffrey!"

The trip to Miami was successful. William Thompson agreed to stand beside his friend, Jeffrey Brooks, when the fight between David Clawson and Sam Kasserman reached the boardroom. Then Natalie's uncle quietly went around, sounding out the other members of the board of directors. She admired the smooth way the wily old financier operated.

Once he was sure of his support on the board, Jeffrey got Sam Kasserman cornered and elicited his promise to resume production of *The Last Encounter* in exchange for having a majority of the board behind him in his conflict with David Clawson.

The fight was over before it began. A special board meeting was held. Clawson left the room shaken and defeated. The majority of the stockholders were solidly behind Sam Kasserman. For David Clawson, the handwriting was on the wall. His days at Atlantic Enterprises were numbered. He resigned.

Natalie was elated. She immediately phoned her friends in Hollywood. There was a cheer of elation. They had been under a cloud of despair for weeks. Now the sun had burst through. Continental Films approved a new budget. Work on the space sets was resumed.

The big problem was locating Kirk Trammer. He had apparently vanished from the face of the earth. It took two weeks for Bill Dentmen to track him down. He eventually found Kirk in a little dirt-floor *cantina* in Matamores, Mexico, drowning his sorrow. Bill sobered him up and they took the next plane to Hollywood.

There were several more months of hard work, shooting the outer space sequences. Then the film went into its post-production phase, which could take as long as the actual filming. In the cutting room, the final version of the story would really take place as the film editor pored over countless feet of film, choosing the scenes to be used. The musical score had to be adapted to the edited film.

Natalie's work on the film was over. She accepted a role in a movie being shot for TV in Wyoming. As she was packing to leave, she got an unexpected call from her attorney. "Miss Brooks, we've got some news you've been waiting to hear. All of the problems relating to your divorce have been ironed out. We're ready for the court hearing."

Natalie felt a strange kind of cold shock. Yes, she had been waiting for this call. Now that the time had come she found herself less prepared than she had believed. "So—so soon?" she stammered.

"Yes. It's been smooth sailing right down the line. Most of the delay was in contacting Kirk. He's been so wrapped up in that film he's producing. However, he's making no demands as far as property settlement is concerned."

"That—that hardly seems fair. He put a lot of money into that big house we own."

"Yes, but he readily admitted he sank his share of the assets the two of you had accumulated into his film, *The Two of Us,* that lost so much money. He's making no claim on any property presently owned and will sign a quitclaim deed to the house. Since you're not asking for alimony, and it's an uncontested, no-fault divorce, there's not much for you to do except appear in court and the decree will be granted."

"When will we do that?"

"It's set up for this week. We thought you'd want to have it settled before you leave for Wyoming."

"Yes . . . all right," Natalie said.

She felt strangely disoriented and lonely as she put the phone down. Tears trickled down her cheeks. From a logical, rational standpoint, she knew it had to end this way. Yet, it was the end of a lot of dreams and hopes that had started out so bravely. She thought that divorce was a bleak reality, the sad ending of a fairy-book love story.

When she drove to the airport on Friday, it was over. She and Kirk were no longer married. She told herself there was no difference, really, no need for the feeling of loneliness that engulfed her. She had been alone in a physical sense since that time Kirk had deserted her and gone off to Europe. Yet, there had been a kind of unseen spiritual bond because they were still legally married. Deep down, there had flickered a faint hope that a miracle might bring them back together. But Kirk had remained cold and aloof during the remainder of time they worked on *The Last Encounter.* He had treated her with the impersonal professional attitude of a director relating to an actress. He'd obviously reached the same conclusion that their marriage was best ended.

Now she was a single woman again. She realized she was facing a period of readjustment.

The Last Encounter had its premier early the following summer. It fulfilled everybody's dreams. The reviews were superlative. "This is the year's Big One. . . Stunning cinematography and effects . . . a moving story . . . manages to entertain while achieving artistic excellence. . . . Powerful drama . . ."

Sam Kasserman was jubilant. Rentals from movie houses around the country poured in. Critics raved. Audiences formed long lines. It was the blockbuster of the year, as Kirk had predicted. Then came the Academy Award nominations. Natalie and Tom Sacks for best leads. Marsha Sanders for best supporting actress. The movie itself for best movie of the year. Other nominations included best director, best special effects, best musical score.

Natalie had completed the made-for-TV movie in Wyoming and was working on a film in Ireland when the date for the Academy Awards rolled around. She took a break in her schedule and flew to Hollywood for the event. She had closed up the big house in Beverly Hills and put it on the market, so she stayed with her cousin, Ginny Wells.

Tom Sacks was her escort to the evening of Academy Awards. She hadn't seen Tom since the completion of the movie. Both had been working on productions in different parts of the world. Tom's gaze lit up when he picked her up that night. He grinned. "Well, are you all set to pick up your Oscar?"

"I'm not quite that confident," she replied. "But it's an honor just to be nominated. This is the first time I've gotten this close."

"Well, same for me," he admitted. "I have Kirk's directing to thank for getting me this nomination. Several times while we were shooting the film, I felt like taking a swing at him, but when I saw myself on the screen, really acting for the first time in my career, I took my hat off to the guy."

Natalie looked away, hiding the emotion stirred by the mention of Kirk's name.

When they were in Tom's car on the way to the auditorium, he said, "Natalie, you're still as beautiful as ever. When are we going to get together for a date? You're single now. I told you once before that I thought we'd make a great couple."

"You'll have to fly to Ireland," she quipped. "I'll be on location there for another two months."

"Okay," he said. "I'm going to get my schedule arranged to do just that. We can go out to an Irish pub."

"That sounds like fun," Natalie agreed.

She managed to keep up a light banter, but her

thoughts were on the evening ahead. Kirk would be at the banquet. She was bracing herself for the emotional impact of seeing him again.

They had arranged to sit with Ginny Wells, the Dentmens and Linda Towers. Linda had done the editing on the film. Natalie's agent, Ira Bevans, was there, as was Sam Kasserman and others who had been close to the production. Natalie waved to them and to numerous Hollywood stars and celebrities that she knew. At first she didn't see Kirk. Then she caught sight of him sitting with a group some distance away. Marsha Sanders was beside him. She felt a familiar sharp stab of pain. During the past months she had thrown herself into her work, concentrating all her energy on the role she was playing. The hurting memories had dulled somewhat. She thought she was getting it all out of her system, but seeing Kirk again tonight brought back a rush of mingled emotions as painful as ever.

Kirk didn't see her. He and Marsha had their heads together, talking earnestly, oblivious to anyone around them.

Then the auditorium lights softened and the glamorous event got underway.

Suspense mounted as the hours passed and nominations and awards were made. Oscars for *The Last Encounter* began piling up. Best cinematography. Best musical score. The Dentmens were awarded top honors for best screenplay.

Ginny squealed when she won top award for best special effects. Tears were streaming down her cheeks when she made her acceptance speech. "I just wish my dad were still with us," she said. "He was the greatest in the business. He taught me everything I know. Dad, this is for both of us," she choked.

Then came awards for supporting roles. "The winner of best supporting actress award—Marsha Sanders for her role of Nichole Nikova in *The Last Encounter.*" The audience responded with a burst of applause. Natalie felt a wrench of emotion as she watched the beautiful, dark-eyed girl leave her place beside Kirk to accept her prize. Was she living with Kirk now? Would they be married soon? Natalie tried to push the unbearable thoughts away.

When it was time to make the award for top director, an actress on the stage opened the envelope, paused and then exclaimed, "Best director—Kirk Trammer for his work on *The Last Encounter!*"

There was another sweep of applause through the auditorium. "Well, I have to admit he deserves it," Tom Sacks muttered.

Through a haze of tears, Natalie saw Kirk stride to the podium. She was surprised at the rush of warmth and pride she felt for Kirk.

In his brief acceptance speech, he said, "This award belongs to all the people who worked so hard with me on the film. Natalie Brooks, we owe special thanks to you. Without you *The Last Encounter* never would have made it to the theaters."

He was looking across the room, straight at her when he said the words. She was riveted to her seat as if impaled by his flashing look. She was barely aware of the murmur that ran through the audience or the dozens of eyes turned in her direction.

The moment left her dazed and weak. She had expected that seeing Kirk again would be an emotional ordeal. But she had not been prepared for this total devastation of her defenses. Kirk had done it again—left her emotions in ruins.

She was almost relieved that she did not receive the award for best actress. She doubted if her legs would have taken her to the stage. Tom was less gracious about missing his chance. "Damn!" he muttered under his breath when another actor topped him for the coveted award.

The evening came to a climax with the announcement of the winning movie of the year. There was little doubt in the audience as to what it would be. "Best picture of the year—*The Last Encounter.*"

This time the applause was thunderous. Around Natalie, pandemonium broke loose. There was laughter, tears, hugs, kisses and handshakes.

Somewhere in the hysteria of the moment, Natalie felt a firm hand on her arm. She turned and looked up into a pair of flashing hazel eyes. Her knees went weak. She swallowed hard and managed to find her voice.

"Congratulations, Kirk," she said.

Suddenly, all the people around them dissolved into a vague backdrop. There were only the two of them, Kirk's hands on his arms, his eyes looking into hers, draining the strength from her body. A slow smile crossed his lips. Then he bent and kissed her gently.

Natalie's breath was a sob catching in her throat.

Then Kirk vanished in the crowd.

Later that evening there was a triumphant party at the palatial Hollywood mansion of Sam Kasserman. The guest list read like a roster of Hollywood's top stars, directors, studio executives and agents.

Again Natalie was surrounded by a crush of friends and well-wishers. She felt as if she were on an emotional high, somewhere between hysterical laughter and tears. The voices, drinks and excitement were making her head swim.

She had been looking around the room since she arrived but hadn't seen Kirk. Then, suddenly she felt the familiar firm grip on her arm. He had seemed to appear from nowhere. With his hand on her arm, he extracted her from a cluster of guests.

"Can we get away from this mob for a talk?" he asked, holding her captive with his eyes.

For a moment she was taken by surprise. She didn't know what to say. But his intense look searched deeply into her eyes with hypnotic force, making the decision for her. "I—I guess so," she stammered.

They slipped through French doors to the veranda. From there, steps led down to a formal garden. They walked along a graveled path and paused near a pool where a fountain splashed softly. Natalie took a seat on a bench. Kirk leaned against a tree, arms folded. His face was in darkness, but she could feel the force of his gaze.

The sound of the party in the big house was muffled and distant. They were surrounded by the perfume of garden plants and flowers. Above them, the stars and a full moon twinkled through the trees.

"How've you been, Natalie?" Kirk asked.

"All right," she said, feeling acutely self-conscious. "Keeping busy. How have you been?"

He shrugged noncommittally.

Natalie felt a rush of a thousand poignant memories, all the times good and bad that they had shared.

For the past year she had buried the memories but they were surfacing now. There was no way to completely erase the years one had shared with another person. The memories brought a medley of mixed emotions—the sweetness of when she first fell in love with him darkened with the bitterness of the way it had ended.

Natalie realized her palms were damp. She pressed them against her skirt. "Kirk, I want to congratulate you again. You deserve to be honored for your achievement. You gave part of your life to that film."

"Thank you," he said quietly. "I meant what I said from the stage. The film would never have been completed without you. I didn't find out exactly what you did in New York, but I know you had something to do with the way Sam Kasserman suddenly changed his mind and went ahead with the production. It was probably involved with your great-uncle Jeffrey being on the board of directors of the parent corporation."

"That's not important. The bottom line is that you had a tremendous motion picture to begin with and you did an outstanding job of producing and directing it. No one else in the industry could have pulled it off the way you did."

"Thank you," he said quietly. "I'd rather hear that from you than have the Oscar. I'm disappointed that you didn't win the Academy Award, though. You should have had it, Natalie. Your portrayal of Rebecca Abrahms was superb, the best thing you've done in your acting career. I think the only reason they didn't give it to you was because *The Last Encounter* won so many awards, they felt obligated to spread some of the top honors around to other people."

"Thanks." She laughed self-consciously. "I remember the battles we had over how I should play the part. I have to tell you this, Kirk—everything you said was right. You brought out the best of me in that part. I'm so glad I got to do Rebecca Abrahms. Maybe they didn't give me the Oscar this year, but I grew a lot in that part. My acting has had a new depth and maturity it never had before. I—I have to give you credit for that."

Kirk didn't reply, but he looked pleased.

They fell silent for several moments. Then Natalie said nervously, "Well . . . I guess I'd better get back to the party—"

He was still regarding her with his searching gaze. "Any regrets, Natalie?" he asked softly.

"What do you mean—?"

"I mean about us. The divorce."

She swallowed hard. "Oh, a few, I guess. A divorce is not something to jump up and down about." Tears were starting to blur her vision. She blinked them back. "It was the only thing to do, though."

"Are you sure?"

"Well, of course. Obviously you agreed. You didn't try to stop me."

"No, I couldn't at that time."

She frowned. What did he mean? She wasn't going to ask him. This conversation was becoming too painful. She rose. "I have to get back to the party."

"Are you really having such a great time in there? You hate parties like that, Natalie."

He was quite right. She actually detested these kinds of extravagant gatherings. She felt self-conscious and uncomfortable making small talk with a lot of people, a hangover from her childhood shyness.

"How about sneaking out and going for a ride with me?"

"Where to?" she asked with a fresh wave of nervousness.

"Down to Long Beach. I bought a boat this week. I'd like to show her to you."

She was conscious of the quickened beating of her heart. She felt confused, her emotions again at war the way they were whenever she was around Kirk. This must be a dream, she thought. She never thought she'd be alone with Kirk again.

"I—I can't leave with you, Kirk. Tom Sacks brought me to the party."

"Do you really want to stick with Tom all evening?" he asked.

She couldn't say yes without lying. Instead, she said, "Won't you make Marsha angry?"

"About what?"

"You leaving the party without her."

"I didn't bring her to the party."

Natalie looked at him with surprise. "You were sitting with her at the Academy Awards."

"No, she was sitting with me."

"What is that supposed to mean?"

"Just what it sounds like. I was there with friends and she joined us."

Natalie pressed her throbbing temples. Kirk was confusing her. He was good at that. He was smarter than she was. When he started talking, she became unsure and her thoughts floundered and he could talk her into anything.

Now he firmly took her arm, guided her around the house to the area where the guests' cars were parked. He spoke to an attendant who brought up Kirk's car, a low, sleek import.

What am I doing? she asked herself with a wave of panic. She almost turned and ran, but Kirk's firm arm guided her into the car. She sank into plush velour upholstery, her body tense, her icy hands clasped.

Kirk slid behind the wheel. The powerful engine purred. Air conditioning whispered. Music played softly from hidden speakers. He swung out of the driveway.

Natalie stared at his rugged profile dimly illuminated from the dashboard lights. She thought that he was certainly driving an expensive car. Then she realized that with the success of *The Last Encounter*, he could afford a dozen cars like this plus several sailboats. He owned a part of the movie. By the time the film had made the rounds of domestic movie houses a couple of times, then the foreign prints, eventually TV rights plus all the merchandising gimmicks, Kirk was going to be an extremely wealthy man. They were all going to make a lot of money from the film. When Natalie and her friends formed the production company, their contracts gave them a percentage of the film's gross. She could thank her agent, Ira Bevans, for looking out for her interests on that score.

Natalie found it difficult to relax. She had a sense of

unreality about this strange situation. What was she doing, riding around with her ex-husband? She had no business being here.

They made the trip to Long Beach in silence. Finally, he stopped the car. Looking around, she realized they had driven to the waterfront.

He helped her out of the car. She gathered the hem of her long dress around her as they walked down the docks. He pointed to a boat anchored in the harbor. "There she is," he said.

She gasped, "Kirk, it's beautiful!"

She had expected a thirty-foot sailboat. It was a good deal more than that; it was a comfortable yacht large enough to sail anywhere in the world.

She frowned. "It looks familiar."

"Yes, you've seen her before."

"Where?" she asked, surprised.

"In the harbor in Rio de Janeiro. Remember the financial tycoon who loaned us his yacht for one of the scenes we filmed down there?"

"This is the same yacht!" she exclaimed. "How did you ever get it?"

Kirk laughed. "Very simple. I made him an offer he couldn't refuse. As part of the deal, he brought her through the Panama Canal and up the West Coast and delivered her to me here."

Natalie was speechless. This was beginning to sound like a scene from a movie Kirk would dream up. But why not? Kirk Trammer was inclined to do things in a flamboyant way. Everything he did, from the way he lived to the kinds of movies he directed, was bigger than life.

They rode a tender out to where the yacht was anchored.

"Come aboard."

He helped her up a ladder and led her to a comfortable seat on the deck.

"Be right back," he promised.

He disappeared into the cabin and returned in a moment with a bottle of champagne in a bucket of ice. The cork popped and he poured foaming liquid into two glasses. He handed one to Natalie.

"I have another bottle, not quite as expensive, that I've been saving for the christening."

"Oh? What do you plan to name her?"

His hazel eyes were gazing at her in a direct way that made a chill ripple up her nerve ends. "I've had a name all picked out. Remember that boat we sailed along the southern coast of France that summer after *The Home Front* had its debut?"

Her mouth felt dry. She took a sip of the champagne. "Yes."

"I named her *Natalie.*"

"I—I remember," she said, her voice unsteady.

"Well, I'm going to name this one *Natalie II.*"

Her hand clasping the thin stem of the champagne glass trembled as she put the glass down. "Kirk . . . I—I don't understand . . ."

"Aren't you going to ask why I want to name my boat after you?"

"I—I don't know."

She thought, *I don't know much of anything right now.*

Kirk crossed his long legs, leaning back luxuriously

against the cushions, and gazed up at the full moon through the rigging. "I'm planning to take her on a world cruise," he said casually. "I thought maybe you might like to come along."

Her face paled. Tears blurred her vision. "Kirk, are you trying to get back at me with some kind of cruel joke?"

He looked at her soberly. "It's no joke, Natalie. My films always have a happy ending. I'm trying to write a happy ending for us."

She shook her head in bewilderment. "Kirk, it's too late for us—"

He put down his drink and sat beside her, taking her hand. She started as she felt the powerful surge of vitality from his fingers through her body. "It's not too late, Natalie," he said huskily. "I won't let it be too late. I love you. I want you to be my wife, forever. Do you understand? I'm asking you to marry me again."

She gazed at him in stricken wonder and dismay. "No, I don't understand! Kirk, you never loved me! You are in love with the memory of the only woman you ever loved, Jacqueline Davis." Tears suddenly burned her eyes. She choked. "I don't know why you married me in the first place, or why you came back from Europe to make me miserable." Then in a wave of anger, she cried, "Yes, I do! You wanted to make *The Last Encounter* and I was your ticket to studio backing! Now what do you want me for?" she demanded bitterly. "You have everything—success, money, acclaim. . . ."

She tried to pull her hands from his grasp, but he held them firmly. He gazed soberly into her eyes.

"Natalie, listen to me. Much of what you say is true. Yes, when I married you I was still hung up on Jacqueline. You accused me of making *The Two of Us* to bring her back to life. You were partly right. I had to make that film to live over that chapter of my life and put the memory of Jacqueline to rest. I've done that, believe me. The reason I left you and went to Europe was because you were making a success of your career and I was a miserable failure. I just couldn't hang around the house, letting you support me. When I was in Europe, I put together my ideas for *The Last Encounter*. I wanted this one to be your film, Natalie. Believe me, I had no intention of using you just to get studio backing. But I was desperate. When that seemed the only way we were going to do the picture, I compromised and took it on those terms. I felt justified in doing it because I believed it was the only hope I had of getting you back. I couldn't ask you to be my wife again unless I could prove myself. I had to wait until I was certain *The Last Encounter* would be a rousing success before I could beg you to come back to me. Can you understand what I'm trying to tell you?"

Natalie felt weak from the flood of emotions that threatened to drown her. She pulled her hands from Kirk's grasp, pressing them against her burning cheeks. Then she arose and walked to the ship's rail. Tears were streaming down her cheeks as she gazed at the lights of the harbor. "It's—it's too late, Kirk," she choked.

"No it isn't," he said, moving behind her and putting his arms around her. He gently kissed her hair. "I love you, Natalie. And you love me. I can feel your body trembling right now because it's close to mine. You're thinking about that night we made love on the beach in Malibu when I came back from Europe and that night in Tunis. Those times you came to me because you felt sorry for me. I couldn't ask you to come back to me out of pity. Now I don't have to. I know you still love me and want me as much as I want you. We can be lovers on equal terms now, with shared respect and dignity."

He turned her to face him.

She saw him through a blur of tears. "Kirk, no . . ." she whispered unsteadily. But his lips found hers in the darkness and her mouth burned from his kiss.

Her legs had grown weak. He scooped her up and carried her to the deck couch. "Remember that night in Rio?" he whispered softly. "We almost made love on this very couch. I think that was the main reason I had to buy this yacht. We had some unfinished business here."

He kissed her again. She felt the blood begin to pound through her body in heightened waves as he awakened slumbering passions. Soon, she could no longer struggle against mounting desire. Her arms slipped around him and she returned his kisses.

"People like us never have smooth sailing in a marriage," Kirk murmured. "We're too volatile. Our careers will keep getting in the way. We'll fight and separate and make up a hundred times. But we'll always get back together for the simple reason that we can't stay apart."

They made love as the ship rocked gently and the moon faded from the sky.

Natalie slept for a while in Kirk's arms. Dawn was tinging the air with its first pale light when she rose and went to the rail, hugging her arms against the morning chill as she gazed across the water.

She heard Kirk stir behind her.

He said sleepily, "You never did say when we could leave on that world cruise together."

She shook her head slowly, a tear trickling down her cheek. "I can't, Kirk. I'm in the middle of a film. I'm going back to Ireland tomorrow."

There was a long silence. The waves lapped softly at the hull below. A sea gull in search of breakfast swooped over the water and made a cawing sound.

Then she heard Kirk chuckle softly. "Yeah, but you'll be back."

EYE OF THE STORM

MAURA SEGER

A powerful portrayal of the events of World War II in the Pacific, *Eye of the Storm* is a riveting story of how love triumphs over hatred. In this, the first of a three book chronicle, Army nurse Maggie Lawrence meets Marine Sgt. Anthony Gargano. Despite military regulations against fraternization, they resolve to face together whatever lies ahead.... Also known by her fans as Laurel Winslow, Sara Jennings, Anne MacNeil and Jenny Bates, Maura Seger, author of this searing novel, was named by ROMANTIC TIMES as 1984's Most Versatile Romance Author.

At your favorite bookstore in March.

EYE-B-1

Genuine Silhouette sterling silver bookmark for only $15.95!

What a beautiful way to hold your place in your current romance! This genuine sterling silver bookmark, with the distinctive Silhouette symbol in elegant black, measures 1½″ long and 1″ wide. It makes a beautiful gift for yourself, and for every romantic you know! And, at only $15.95 each, including all postage and handling charges, you'll want to order several now, while supplies last.

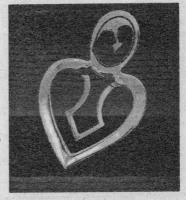

Send your name and address with check or money order for $15.95 per bookmark ordered to

**Silhouette Books
120 Brighton Rd., P.O. Box 5084
Clifton, N.J. 07015-5084
Attn: Bookmark**

Bookmarks can be ordered pre-paid only. No charges will be accepted. Please allow 4-6 weeks for delivery.

N.Y. State Residents
Please Add Sales Tax

READERS' COMMENTS ON SILHOUETTE SPECIAL EDITIONS:

"I just finished reading the first six Silhouette Special Edition Books and I had to take the opportunity to write you and tell you how much I enjoyed them. I enjoyed all the authors in this series. Best wishes on your Silhouette Special Editions line and many thanks."

—B.H.*, Jackson, OH

"The Special Editions are really special and I enjoyed them very much! I am looking forward to next month's books."

—R.M.W.*, Melbourne, FL

"I've just finished reading four of your first six Special Editions and I enjoyed them very much. I like the more sensual detail and longer stories. I will look forward each month to your new Special Editions."

—L.S.*, Visalia, CA

"Silhouette Special Editions are — 1.) Superb! 2.) Great! 3.) Delicious! 4.) Fantastic! . . . Did I leave anything out? These are books that an adult woman can read . . . I love them!"

—H.C.*, Monterey Park, CA

*names available on request